Sunshine ON A CLOUDY DAY

ELLE ROBS

ASPIRE
PUBLISHING HUB LLC.

Sunshine on a Cloudy Day
Copyright © 2025 by Elle Robs

Library of Congress Control Number: 2024927146

ISBN
979-8-89683-053-5 (Paperback)
979-8-89683-054-2 (eBook)
979-8-89683-052-8 (Hardcover)

DEDICATION

To my Here 4 the Girls teams 2024 Calendar Ambassadors. To everyone who fought this disease called Cancer.

Fighting alone is not an option. If you are dealing with Breast Cancer, please go to https://hereforthegirls.org/ This organization has been great with assisting me with finding my voice in the storm called Cancer.

Table of Contents

A Cloudy day is no match
for a SUNNY Disposition.

~William Arthur Ward~

The sun shall be no more
thy light by day; neither for
brightness shall the moon
give light unto thee: but
the LORD shall be unto
thee an everlasting light,
and thy God thy glory.

Isaiah 60:19 *KJV*

Some Days you just have to
create your own SUNSHINE.

~Unknown~

Acknowledgements

This book is dedicated to my pen pal and fellow writer, LaShonda Bowman. Girl, our friendship took a course for which I am forever grateful. You are my sister, and I love you.

To my friends Audrey, Olandra, Mrs. Sue, Cicely, DeVonda, and Termeka who stood beside me, thank you for being a part of the force to help me fight this battle. Thank you for everything!

To my real-life Bishop Theotis White, I and Elder Vernerther White. Your support and teaching are why I can stand today.

To my Zion Hopewell family, thank you for all your support.

From praying for me to encouraging me, I thank you.

To my real-life 'David' J. Cole (Not the singer), my husband, Johnny, and his family. Johnny, thank you for never giving up on there being an US. You pursued me for years and I blocked you for years, but I am so glad for that DM on December 8, 2020. Love you

Chapter 1

"Ok, are you ready to turn up for Jesus?" LaShonda screamed in the mic.

The group of youth that had come together for their annual youth conference started to gather at the front of the stage. The church had been transformed from its normal church appearance to a blacked-out club feel. The soft colored walls had been covered in black paper and different messages had been written in neon colors throughout that were only seen when the up lights hit it at the right angle.

It had taken LaShonda and the other youth advisors a full two days to finish it. She knew that they had hit it out of the park from the gasps and screams that came from the youth as they entered the building. The vestibule of the church had been transformed into a selfie station. It was a jeans and t-shirt weekend to keep up with the youthful crowd. Outside of some of the older baby boomers, many of the members had complied, but when Mother Jean Butler came in with her lime green suit with matching hat, LaShonda just had to laugh. The theme was, 'Living in the Limelight of Christ,' and she figured that was Mother Jean's way of being hip, by wearing a lime green suit.

Hearing the children scream snapped LaShonda back into the present. She loved working with the youth and had a special bond with several of them. As a youth leader, she always tried to make sure that she was available for those she deemed as 'her babies.' From attending sport activities to promotion ceremonies, she was there. At almost forty years old, her life was consumed with different activities at the church. If it was not the youth, it was the intercessory team, women's ministry, or singles ministry. If the doors were opened, LaShonda would be there. It sounded bad to others but for LaShonda, it was life. It kept her busy and she loved it. As the children began to chant *yes* and started to get amped up for the event, she knew she had to slow it down and open with prayer.

Then her co-host, Michelle Horry AKA Shell, came on the stage. Shell was the oldest daughter of the Horry clan, and she came in true form as the hype woman.

"Aaaaaaaaaa, Millie Rock!" Shell said as she proceeded to Millie Rock, causing the kids to jump up and join in.

"Girl, you trying to turn up already," LaShonda spoke into the mic.

"It is the Youth Conference. We ain't come to just have a regular church service," Shell says.

A soft murmur of *yes* came from the crowds and the sounds of high fives could be heard.

"We??? Girl, you are not..." Lashonda was abruptly interrupted by Shell.

"Youthfulness is in the eye of the beholder, and I am very youthful, in my own eyes." Shell said as the crowd erupted in laughter.

"Girl, you are a trip, but we got to do one thing before we turn it up a notch."

"What we got to do because I am ready to?" Shell broke out into a series of dance moves, causing the kids to start getting crunk again.

"Before we turn it up, we got to what??" LaShonda turned the mic to the youth and allowed them to finish what had been labeled as her trademark sentence.

"We got to pray it up!" many of the youth shouted. Beaming with joy, LaShonda started laughing.

"Okay, okay. So, who wants to pray?"

When two of her strongest youth prayer warriors stood, she shook her head at them. "No," LaShonda said, "we are going to get someone new today. Eric and Lori, come on up to the stage."

Nervously, the children made their way to the stage after looking around terrified to confirm that it was them that LaShonda had called. LaShonda started to publicize the crowd as they got to the stage...

"Okay, now! We do not pray alone, do we?"

"No," screamed the crowd. "OKAY, so let's join our faith with their faith and let's set the atmosphere for God to rest in this place."

As many of the youth started praising God with a few speaking in tongues, LaShonda knew she was tapping into her purpose. Not having any children of her own, she looked at the babies that stood before her as her children and knew God placed her in a position to not just be a mother to a few but to be a mother to many. While she still held the hope to one day have her own, right now, she knew her singleness and her childlessness were serving a purpose.

As Eric grabbed the mic and started praying, LaShonda was shocked hearing the young man pray. He had been attending the 'How to Pray' workshop that was held every Sunday with all the youth males under twenty-five and it was obvious. As he finished, he handed the mic to Lori. Lori looked at the mic doubtful as though she was about to run off the stage.

Walking beside her, LaShonda bent down and whispered...

"Even if you just say one word, you just give your piece of the sentence."

Lori sighed and took the mic from Eric. Lori opened her mouth to start praying and as she prayed, she started singing. As the children began to worship loudly, Lori released the mic and fell to the floor. The band, who was playing softly in the back, LaShonda motioned for the Praise and Worship team to take stage.

The beginning of the youth conference was starting off right.

Chapter 2

"Man, this year's Youth Conference was amazing!" Brad said to David as they were cleaning up the church.

"You ain't never lied! When the presence of God is tangible, the youngest to the oldest feel it."

David did a two-step before continuing,

"I know that this was something for the youth but that was a revival for the BODY! If you stand still, you can still feel His presence."

Brad watched as David paused in thought and chuckled.

"Yeah well, is He telling you to finally go ask Shonda out on a date?" Brad joked. Snapping out of it, David leaned in Brad's face.

"Yo, shut up. Just shut up!"

"Man, ain't no one here but us! You up there last night singing faith over fear and I wanted to throw my drumstick at you."

"It ain't that easy. I mean Shonda is you know, Shonda…" David said, looking around nervously.

He and Brad quickly became friends when he moved from Atlanta. David remembered that day when he had come up to him right after church and gave him some dap and told him that he knew he had to be hearing from God to move from Atlanta to BORING Columbia, SC. Brad interrupted his thoughts with his next statement.

"Well, you need to do something. I saw how you were staring at her when she was on stage on Friday night. Someone had to hit you to tell you it was time for you to go up on stage."

Looking down at the bag that contained all the decoration that they had taken down since service was over, he replied.

"Is it that obvious? I am trying, but it is like Shonda is not feeling it. Man, I feel like I am playing dodgeball with her at times," David said.

"All I am going to say if you keep that up you are about to be in Lustville… Wait, you are already there," Brad said and started to laugh.

Pushing him in the back, David walked past Brad.

"It is not that easy. I mean Shonda is a woman of God, and if it were not for Casey, I would think maybe she goes the other way," David truthfully admitted.

Casey was LaShonda's best friend who told him to break down the wall that she had put up.

"Look, Shonda is knocking on forty. I am sure she is ready for someone to come scoop her out of her singleness. I mean in reality, she is about to be the oldest single lady in the church," Brad said while picking up a piece of paper off the floor and stuffing it into the trash bag.

"No, Mary still single," David said, thinking about the older church sister who was in her fifties and at one time had set her eyes on him.

After making the mistake of saying his favorite dessert was peach cobbler at one of the singles meetings, she had started bringing peach cobbler to the church every Sunday for him. Thinking about the lady and how persistent she was sent shivers up his spine.

"Where have you been? That cat that had on that blue sugar daddy's suit on last Sunday is her man," Brad said, placing air quotes in the air.

"No! Not Playa-Playa!"

"From the Himalayas!" Brad joked.

Both Brad and David burst out laughing. After getting themselves back together, Brad looked at David.

"I guess she found someone else that likes her peach cobbler."

"I was just thinking about that. I had to talk to the First Lady about her. She would not leave me alone. You know, she came to my job one day," David said while simultaneously shaking his head.

"Yo, you ain't tell me that!"

Brad looked at David, expecting to hear what had happened. When David let out a long sigh, Brad knew it was about to be crazy whatever he was about to say.

"Hold on, let me sit down and hear this."

Brad sat down in one of the chairs in the front of the church and David settled across from him, taking a seat on the stage.

"Man, she found out that I was working at the pharmacy on 14th Street. One day around lunchtime she comes in, in a tight-fitting red dress."

"Isn't red your favorite color?" Brad asked David.

"Yeah, on Shonda. I mean Shonda looks good in everything but yellow and red. Those *are* her colors," David said, wishfully thinking.

"Okay, come back to earth, David… I need to hear the rest of this story," Brad stated. Snapping out of its David continues his story.

"See, the week before, she had heard me telling Shonda about her red dress. Here she comes in this fitted dress. Carrying a Fire House's bag and some peach cobbler. Talking about she thought I might be hungry."

"Ms. Mary was going to get you!" Brad said while trying to hold his laughter in.

"After that, I called First Lady Glenda, and she told me she would handle it. I do not know what she said but Mary has been rolling her eyes at me since. It is no wonder she acted like she did not see me the other Sunday now. Ole Sugar Daddy had her attention."

Brad tried to pull himself back together after falling out laughing about Ms. Mary rolling her eyes at him. He could see David was thinking about the same thing and was looking like he had just tasted the worst type of food possible on Earth.

"Man, all I am saying you turned forty last year, so I definitely need you to handle your business. You up here acting like a schoolboy who never asked anyone out before," Brad teased.

"I want to, but I just don't feel like it is right yet."

"Well," Brad said, standing up. "You do you, but I am about to head out. I have a date... I mean a prayer call meeting with Jessica."

"You are talking about me. But you have been having a prayer call meeting with Jessica for over two years. When are you going to propose?"

"I would say when you ask Shonda out but that's not going to happen anytime soon, so." Brad looked around before he got up to move closer to David.

"I am going to do it next month on her birthday. I asked her parents today for permission and they said yes."

David watched as Brad pulled out the ring box that was in his pocket and pulled Brad into an embrace.

"I am so happy for you man."

"Thanks, I knew Jessica was the one and thanks to Shonda, my proposal is going to be.

FIRE!"

"Shonda?"

"Yes, she is helping me plan it. She is really good at this stuff."

"Cool, so what is the plan?"

Brad proceeded to tell him how they had rented out a movie theatre and Shonda and some of her friends had gotten together and filmed a short film about their relationship. Jessica's and his family would fill the theatre the day of the proposal.

"That is going to be fire!" David agreed, shaking his head in agreement with his friend.

"I know, I am so nervous, but I love her. I cannot imagine my life without her." David dapped Brad up and pulled him into another embrace.

"I am happy for you."

"Thanks. Now you know this is your official invitation, right?" Brad told him as he looked at David.

"I wouldn't miss it," David fist bumped Brad up once more.

Brad looked down at his watch and noticed the time.

"We can finish this up tomorrow. I do not want to make Jessica wait any longer. Confessions of a Hangry Woman is real if she does not eat by 5 pm."

Laughing, both men fist pounded each other. As Brad got ready to leave LaShonda came from the back, talking with Bishop Horry.

"Okay, Bishop, thank you for the insight and I am glad so many of the youth came out to the conference this year." LaShonda could be heard talking to Bishop Horry.

"Yes, Shonda, hold that thought for a minute. Brad, are you leaving?" Bishop Horry called.

"Yes, me and David are going to finish up tomorrow."

"Okay, thank you Brad," Bishop Horry said as Brad exited through the side door to go in the back-parking lot of the church. He then turned his attention back to David.

"Hello, David," Bishop Horry spoke to David.

"Hey, Bishop and Hello, Shonda."

"Hey, David. Well Bishop, I am about to go. I have to go to work in the AM," LaShonda notified.

"Ok, get some rest," Bishop Horry said to her as Lashonda turned to head in the same direction that Brad had just left out of but not before turning her attention to David.

"Thank you and bye, David," LaShonda offered shyly.

Looking at LaShonda, he noticed a slight blush rising across her cheeks. *Did I just make her blush? Did I?* The question ran across his mind several times.

"Bye, Shonda. Actually, I should walk you out." David suggested while getting up from where he sat on the stage.

"No, that is ok. It is still daylight out." LaShonda tried to hurry to the door.

Bishop clearing his throat got both of their attention.

"Yes. That is a fine idea. David, you will walk Shonda out and yes, you will accept this young man's assistance, Shonda."

As he sat down in the sanctuary, Bishop studied the two young people before him. He was aware of David's attraction to LaShonda and LaShonda's rejection of David at every turn.

"I will be right here, David. Go ahead and walk her out and then come back. I need to talk to you."

"Yes, Sir." David turned to face LaShonda and gestured to the door. "After you."

LaShonda knew she would be fighting a losing battle if she told them that she did not need an escort. Letting out a deep sigh, LaShonda headed to the doors of the church.

"Thank you." LaShonda quickly said as she saw David picking up the pace to walk beside her.

She knew David was interested in her and maybe in another lifetime, they would be perfect together, but she had too many skeletons in her closet to bring anyone in. She tried to put distance between them anytime he was near, however, it was getting more difficult to do so. Especially with several people in the church liking to play match maker, including Bishop Horry.

"So, Shonda, I just want to say you did an awesome job with the Youth Conference tonight," David quickened his pace to match hers.

"Glory be to God! I love my babies, and I get such a joy seeing them tap into their purpose and standing confident declaring the Word of God."

As LaShonda continued to talk, David realized that was the subject to break the ice with her. When it came to the ministry, her passion always spilled out.

"David, did you hear what I just said?"

LaShonda had stopped walking and if it was not for her alerting him, he was about to walk dead into her.

"I am sorry I did not. I was thinking about how whatever you said to little Lori just opened her up. I never heard her talk that much, no less talking about praying."

Laughing, LaShonda knew that it shocked everyone to hear Lori pray, but she knew that it was in her. She just needed a little help with getting it out of her.

"We all have a piece to the sentence," LaShonda said.

"Huh?" David said, looking at her confused.

"I told her that we all have a piece of the sentence. Even if it just one word, give your piece to the sentence."

"That is some good advice. I am going to have to remember that the next time I minister.

You know I will give you credit every once and a while." David opened the doors to the parking lot, allowing LaShonda to go out.

LaShonda walked out chuckling, "You are funny."

Walking up to her SUV she disarmed the alarm and paused, allowing him the chance to open the door for her.

"Thank you, David, for walking me to my car. I better let you get back into the church so you can talk to Bishop Horry." LaShonda tried to rush and get into her car.

"Yeah, I enjoyed our conversation. Maybe…"

LaShonda quickly squeezed his hand and said, "I been at this church since eight this morning, I am ready to get home."

"Of course." David tried not to sound defeated. "I will see you at Bible Study."

He closed the door to her car and stepped back to watch her start her car up and pull off. When he made sure she had safely exited the parking lot, he turned around and headed back to the church. He knew LaShonda had blocked him. In fact, her nickname around the single men at church was Ice Queen. So many dudes had tried to talk to her, and she had avoided them all.

Many speculated if she was even into men, David already knew that was not the case.

He knew that LaShonda just did not fool a bunch of people. Jogging back to the church, he shook his head and started laughing. He just knew he was the right element to melt that wall of ice that she had built up.

Chapter 3

Bishop Horry sat there watching David as he reentered into the church. "You are back quick; she must have blocked you."

David stopped and laughed, already knowing Bishop Horry was about to clown him. "Bishop, I tried!"

"Is that what you called it? You 'tried'? I think you should try that again." "Bishop, come on! Every time I try to talk to her, she..."

"Cuts you off?" Bishop Horry stated, finishing David's sentence.

"Yes, and I'm not sure what else to do." David said, sounding exasperated.

"I am going to share this with you, and it is only because she has shared it with the congregation prior and with the youth prior to you joining here. Do you know how Shonda ended up here at this church?"

He continued after seeing David shake his head *no*.

"Shonda was a sophomore at BenU. I was the school Chaplin there at the time. One of her professors called me, asking me did I have any ties with anywhere that could house her over the summer."

Bishop Horry noted the display of emotions that went across David's face and realized this was new information for him. Sighing, he sat up and continued his story.

"Shonda grew up in foster care. During the summer break of her second year, her foster parents told her that she could not come home. Because Shonda went to school, her foster family was still getting a check for her until she turned twenty-one. But when the checks stopped, they did not have a reason to get her."

"What? That is horrible. I cannot even imagine what I would do if that would have happened to me." David looked up at Bishop with a disdained look on his face. "What happened?"

"I remember Shonda coming to my office that day in tears. She was ashamed that she was sitting there with no place to go. My heart broke for her. I called and talked to the First Lady, and we made the decision to allow her to stay in our house. She was almost the same age as our children, and we had just rented out the last of our rental properties. She stayed with us and in a short amount of time she became close with our kids and the next thing we knew; it was as though Shonda was part of our family."

"That's awesome."

"Yes, for many of our holidays, Shonda still eats dinner with us." "Where is Shonda's foster family?"

"Right there in Dansville."

"What? That is like thirty minutes away."

"When they needed her, she used to go flying down there ready to help. Even though she has gotten a lot better over the years, she still confuses being *needed* with being *loved*. Even today, I find myself telling her, 'Daughter, stop it and let someone else do it.'"

"She is involved in a lot of church activities."

"Do not get me started on that and let me finish my story. Christmas's break that same year, Shonda wanted to go home. So, they got her."

David continued to give Bishop his undivided attention, as he felt in his heart the story was about to take a turn for the worst.

"Christmas went without a hitch," Bishop Horry continued. "Her birthday is right after Christmas, so we called Shonda to tell her Happy Birthday. When we called her, she did not sound right, and while we were asking what was wrong, we started hearing her foster mother in the background. She was spewing so many hateful things at her and calling her all out of her name."

Bishop Horry paused in telling the story to David. This part of the story LaShonda had never shared with the congregation, but he also knew David needed to know this before really deciding to go after LaShonda.

"Then we heard something like it was being thrown and then Shonda panting and running. I told Shonda she did not have to deal with that and that we were coming to get her. When me and Glenda got to her foster family's house, Shonda was standing outside. We pulled up and was helping her get into the car when her foster mother came running outside with a gun."

"A GUN?!" David said, looking at Bishop Horry shocked.

"Yes, Shonda jumped in the van, and we sped off." Stopping the story, Bishop Horry looked up to the sky and then started laughing.

"Bishop, are you okay?" David asked.

"Yeah, I was thinking how I sped away. I always loved watching *Dukes of Hazzard* but, on that day..." Bishop said, taking a small pause and looking at David with tears in his eyes. "I could have been on *Dukes of Hazzard*. I had that van in the air and there was a small railroad crossing and I sho' nuff jumped it!"

David and Bishop both fell out laughing as they both took time to envision the moment.

"I tell you; I can look back and laugh at that now but back then I was mad. That woman put my wife, myself, and Shonda at risk with that stunt. I could not even imagine how Shonda had.

even grown up into the woman that she was, living in a hell like that." Bishop was no longer laughing and had an angry expression scowled over his face.

David was shocked how angry Bishop had gotten. He had seen Bishop angry before but not like this. The hurt of what LaShonda's foster mom had done was still evident.

"Do you know she told Shonda that she tried to shoot but bullets weren't in the gun? When she saw Shonda getting in the car, she just ran out of the house, thinking the gun was already loaded."

"No one tried to put her away to get help?" David asked seriously.

"No, her husband is a whipped man. He loves his wife and even though he knows what she was doing to Shonda was wrong, he would not or could not do anything to get the woman help. That woman needs some serious help."

David immediately shook his head in agreement. "I haven't heard of anything like this before and I volunteer at the group home."

"I remembered her sitting in the back of that van, crying silent tears all the way back to the house. We took her to get something to eat so that the other children would not see her so upset. See, her foster mom is not wrapped too tight. Shonda started telling us how when she was younger, her foster mom would come in her room and start accusing Shonda of bringing people into her house or that she was sleeping with people. It was to the point that Shonda could not even have a door to her room. She was only allowed a curtain."

"Jesus!" David stood up and started pacing. Bishop stopped speaking to allow David a moment to comprehend everything he had said. When David stopped pacing, he turned and looked at Bishop, "the saying is right. No one really knows what is hidden behind a person's smile."

"You are correct, son." Bishop Horry said, smiling at David's revelation.

"What happened to make her foster mom flip so hard on her that day?"

Bishop let out a long sigh before continuing the story.

"On that day, Shonda's foster father gave her some money for her birthday. Her foster mother saw it and started accusing Shonda of doing something disgusting for the money. Shonda used to write poetry and short stories. Her mom found her books and started to ridicule her, called some of her friends on the phone, and read her poems to her friends, allowing them to laugh at her, and then when the ridicule didn't get the desired results, she threw all of Shonda's poetry books in the trash."

"Bishop..."

"Shonda made the mistake of going and trying to dig them out of the trash can when her mom came behind her and hit her. Shonda said she did not know with what, but she remembers turning around, looking at her foster mom, and seeing a look that made her scared, so she ran into her room. That was right before we called. She said that she picked up the phone, thinking that her mom normally did not act out when it was a possibility of someone hearing it, but on that day she did not care. She picked up a box and threw it at her, which caused her to run."

"I can't believe this." David said, while shaking his head back and forth.

"David, she came back with us and stayed with us during that break and from that point on. She refused to live with us during the school year. She continued to stay on campus, and we would have to beg her to come home at least once a month. She attended church with us and went out to eat with us on Sunday after church, but she pretty much was independent. She worked hard and graduated a year earlier and started on her master's. When she finished her master's in social work, she already had a job lined up."

"Shonda is quite a woman but Bishop… why did you tell me all of this?" Looking at him inquisitively, David waited for Bishop to answer him.

When Bishop got up and started walking to the door, he paused halfway to the door, turned back around, and looked at David.

"In order to melt ice, you need fire." Seeing the shocked look on David's face, Bishop Horry smiled.

"Yes, I know what they call her. Shonda is not made up of ice, but she is a woman who has never really had anyone looking out for her. In her head, she has always had to be fifty steps ahead. That is why she is good at strategic management. Give her ten minutes with a problem, she will map it out for you."

David continued to stare at Bishop Horry as he continued with what he thought was an inside joke amongst the men at the church.

"David, to understand Shonda and know why she does the things she does, you are going to not only have to melt the ice around her but also the ice around her past. She is very guarded. Even after twenty years, she is still guarded with us. But I assure you, if you can melt that ice, she will give you a love that you never have experienced before." David shook his head and smiled.

"Thank you, Bishop."

"No problem, and David?"

"Yes sir?"

"I told you this so that you can understand who you are dealing with. It is not that Shonda does not find you attractive; it is more that she does not think she deserves you. Now, you have a good evening. First Lady got some peach cobbler waiting on me."

David immediately stopped laughing.

"You said First Lady made some peach cobbler?"

Bishop stopped in the doorway but did not even bother to turn around.

"I told Glenda not to bring her peach cobbler to this church. Now I cannot even mention it without people looking for an invite. Bring your big head on, son."

David did a victory dance before running behind Bishop. Today just went from good to GREAT in David's eyes.

Chapter 4

She waved as the horn beeped and closed her door as the car drove off. LaShonda was still fuming at how she was in the kitchen helping Momma Glenda in the kitchen when she saw Bishop's SUV pull up in the driveway. She was rolling out the rolls when she saw David's car pull up behind Bishop. Rolling her eyes heavenward, she knew Bishop did not forget that she was going to be there today. Every third Sunday, her, Michael Jr., Daniel, Kathryn, and Michelle all got together and ate dinner at their house. Everyone was always picking at her about David so she knew the group chat would be lit tonight at dinner and after.

Entering the door of her home LaShonda quickly turned around and waved at the car that was waiting on her to enter her house. Daniel had suggested that David follow her home to make sure that she got home safely. She silently promised to follow through with the threat that she had sent Daniel earlier. The next time he asked for a sweet potato pie or candied yams she was not going to do it for him.

She knew that was a lie the first time she texted it. She loved Daniel and they shared a special bond. He often came to her house in the evening to chill and watch TV. Daniel was adopted by the Horry when he was twelve, but he had been living with them since he was eight years old. His mother had had a nervous breakdown and tried to kill him and her. The neighbor ran in and saved Daniel when he saw the blaze but was unable to save his mother. It was reported that when the neighbor tried to save her, she fought him and would not let him save her, running deeper into the house where he could not reach her. The neighbor grabbed Daniel and ran out the door just as the apartment exploded.

When Daniel had come to the Horry, LaShonda had just moved in with them. Daniel was almost nine. He was really malnourished and had suffered both physical and mental abuse from his mother. Daniel would just sit there on some days, too scared to move. Understanding him, LaShonda automatically fell in love with Daniel and would force him to talk to her and even go to the store with her. Soon, it was not a question of whether the car cranked up and she was driving, Daniel was in the passenger seat. He often had nightmares at night, which he told no one about until one night it was really bad. Daniel came into LaShonda's room, crying. He had started to remember the fire. LaShonda remembered the many nights where she rocked him back to sleep after he came to her room crying.

Daniel had been labeled as her baby. Everywhere LaShonda went, Daniel was right there and even now he still showed up at her house unannounced and would even sometimes get in bed with her just to talk. LaShonda always knew when Daniel was fighting with his past, because he would lean on her even more. It was the reason that wherever she went, she always let him know that he had a room at her house.

Hearing her phone ring brought LaShonda back to the shenanigans that happened at dinner. She looked at the caller id to see it was one of her best friends that she grew up with, Traci.

"Hey, girl! What is up?"

"Nothing, was just seeing how you're doing."

She and Traci stayed on the phone for an hour before she hung up with her to get ready for the next day when it dawned on her that she had taken that Monday off. After taking a quick shower, she sat on her bed thinking about the evening's events.

✻

❧ EARLIER… DINNER AT MOMMA GLENDA'S

Everyone in their little clique thought her and David would be good together. LaShonda had long ago settled in her head that she was not marriage material. In her eyes, no one wanted her – she was like that gift that you got that you really did not want but you accepted it because you had been taught to be polite. So, you took it knowing it was going to be set aside to collect dust. Yes, she had been in relationships throughout the years, but none of them stayed. They always started off great, and then somehow, they always ended up leaving her. Some had even turned abusive. LaShonda shook her head to stop the memories that were trying to creep into her mind. Looking down at the biscuits she was rolling out, she tried to keep the tears from falling as she thought about the last relationship.

❋

Michael cleared his throat and placed his arm around his date, Denise.

"Daniel, which is a clever idea that David follows Shonda home. I either follow Denise home or talk to her all the way home to make sure she gets home safely."

LaShonda noted Kathryn and Michelle nodding in agreement through her instantly narrowed eyes. She took a large gulp of the lemonade that she was drinking and sat the glass on the table to stare directly at Michael and Daniel.

"That is not necessary. I have been eating here every third Sunday and seeing myself home simply fine for years," she said, thinking she had successfully adverted anyone having to follow her home. She picked up her fork to take another piece of the peach cobbler when Kathryn spoke up.

"Well, we are normally already home by now but because of the youth conference, we started dinner later than normal. It is already getting dark, and we have not even finished this round of Phase 10."

LaShonda sighed, thinking she should have known that it was not going to be as easy as she thought.

"I will be ok. It is not like I have not had to drive home by myself before. It really is not that big of a deal," she said as she completed another phase by laying the cards on the table and throwing out another card. "And besides, me and David both have been at the church since early this morning, so…"

"I don't mind," David said, cutting LaShonda off. He nodded his thanks to Daniel before he continued. "I don't have an issue with making sure you get home safe."

"Like I said I don't need an escort home." Turning her cards over and getting up from the table. "I will get home safely."

Everyone watched as LaShonda got up from the table to take her plate and cup to the kitchen. Michael waited until she was out of earshot to throw a chip at David. "Man, you got to come strong with Shonda. We can only do so much!"

"What I am supposed to do, force her?"

An unanimously 'Yes' came from the table with even Bishop and Momma Glenda joining in.

"With Shonda, you cannot even give her an option. It has to be *I am going to,*" Kathryn said, with people shaking their head in agreement.

"You remember a couple of years back when Shonda had emergency surgery?"

"Yes."

"She was talking about going home after an appendectomy when she could barely move. She just wanted to go home. Daddy had to go up and tell her *'No, this is where you are going to stay for at least a week.'*" Michael started chuckling.

"Daddy and Mommy are the only two with whom she does not argue. Well, she does not argue with me as much. Normally, if they say something, it is law, but she will try them or conveniently leave out stuff and tell them after the fact," Michael said, while looking to make sure LaShonda was still away in the kitchen. "I mean, I still feel as though we didn't get the full story on that Joe character."

"Yes, she definitely didn't tell us the entire story on that one," Shell started.

But before she could finish her thought, Michael, Daniel, Trina, and Kathryn's phones started to buzz simultaneously.

"Oh Lord, which is what was taking so long. She was sending us a text," Michael said.

7:57 pm - Shonda

I cannot believe you all. I am so DONE with this mess. I want you all to know that your Day will come, and Daniel keep boosting David up and see the next time you text me to cook. something, it will not happen. I cannot believe you all. Stop trying to set me and David up!

7:59 - Shell

Girl, stop sending us threats and get your tail back in here.

7:59 – Daniel

Yes, and do not be threatening me with my food. I love you and I really mean it. It was Michael's idea.

8:01 – Michael

Really bro! Spoken just like a fat boy! Ready to lie when food is at stake.

8:01 pm - Daniel

Speak for yourself, you know I am still in school and plus… I sure could use a sweet potato pie.

8:02 pm – Trina

Where are you? You have been gone for a minute!

8:02 pm - Shonda

I am in the back yard. I need a break from all of your matchmaking attempts. I will be. back in a few.

As LaShonda was coming back into the living room, she heard Michael and Shell's comments about Joe. She quickly turned around and headed to the backyard and sat on the swing where she let silent tears flow. They were right; she had not told them everything. As the memories started flooding her memory, the pain and the shame from the last day Joe was in her life overwhelmed her and a soft cry escaped her lips.

Joe had come into her life like Prince Charming and when he left, he left like a hurricane had torn down everything she had built. While she looked at Joe as being the man that she had prayed for, Joe looked at her as an opportunity. She met Joe at the grocery store and for weeks, Joe showed up at the same time she was at the grocery store in his work clothes. He would always stop and talk to her and ask her what she was cooking for dinner. They only shared idle chit chat for a couple of weeks. Things escalated when he asked where she went to church and the next Sunday, she watched as he walked into the church. That evening he asked her out and it seemed all things were going well; they had gone out a couple of times and were even coming to church together. She should have known something was up when he never wanted to be part of the men fellowships or even talk to Bishop. It was like he had an attitude whenever Bishop came around. She should have seen the signs.

Within a few months Joe had moved several things into her place. Even replacing her TV with the one that was conveniently in the back seat of his car. She should have known then that he was looking for a place to stay. Who kept a flat screen TV in the backseat of their car? She quickly found herself wrapped around Joe's finger. He had moved his things into her spare bedroom. He was in and out of her house all through the day. The job that he said he had, suddenly, he was fired from. The reason behind the firing was him taking off time that he claimed he had to help her when she got sick with the flu. She told him not to worry and she was used to taking care of herself. He would not listen, and she felt honored that someone would take the time to take care of her. She felt responsible for him losing his job and allowed him to be at her house more often. She walked in one day and he had completely transformed her living room with his stuff.

When she walked in after work, he was in her living room playing a game. He would stay and eat dinner with her and then leave for the night. He claimed he was staying with friends until his apartment became open. He did find another job as a forklift driver at a plant but what? happened next LaShonda was never prepared for. One day while cleaning up her house Joe came in wanting her to stop what she was doing and fix him something to eat. When she refused, she found Joe in her face and the sweet, mild-mannered Joe who had gone to church with her was now threatening her. He called her all kinds of names and then, he did something she never saw coming- Joe hit her, knocking her down to the floor. He then grinned as he loosened the belt on his pants and allowed his pants to drop.

LaShonda wiped furiously at her eyes with her shirt sleeve. She was so ashamed of what happened to her: raped in her own house. Joe had been pressuring her to have sex despite explaining to him that she wanted to wait until she got married.

When he finished, he got up and told her he had been glad that she did not trap him into marriage because he would not want to wait to know she was serving up trash. She got up and ran into the bathroom and cried. She had stayed in the bathroom for almost two hours before she came out. When she came out Joe was gone and so was all of his stuff, plus some of her stuff. Blowing her nose, she laid back on the swing, looked up into the sky, and closed her eyes. She sat out just a few more minutes before heading back in. Joe was a narcissist and everything that happened to him was someone else's fault. He was never to blame. Closing her eyes, she allowed the sounds of the night to rest her restless soul.

Chapter 5

G lenda stood in the kitchen looking out in the backyard, watching LaShonda struggle with her own private battle. *"Lord, I know what you are leading me to do but I hope her heart and mind is ready to face her truth."*

While in her prayer closet last week Glenda had heard the Holy Spirit say it was time. After asking for clarification, she knew what He was leading her to do. When Richard had called her and told her about LaShonda's predicament, both her and Richard agreed that she was to be a part of their family. Sighing, she took another sip of the coffee that she had just poured. Hearing the laughter and the jokes that were taking place in the other room, she had given Richard the look to keep them occupied while she handled business. Richard had them wrapped in one of his stories. They would not recognize her absence until she returned.

When Richard came into Glenda's life, she fought him tooth and nail, but he did not let up. He kept being present in her life. She never forgot the day that let her know that she did not need to run *from* him any longer, but she could run *to* him. She recognized he would be the strong tower that would cover her and love her throughout life's happenings. After leaving Michael's father, her and Michael Jr. was staying with her grandmother, Wilhelmina Mary Townsends, whom she affectionately called 'Baby Cake.'

One Sunday while in the church that her and Richard attended, the church administrator had her out of service and when she picked up the phone, it was her grandmother's next-door neighbor, Mary. Mary was crying, saying that they had found her grandmother on the floor in house. Mary's husband also drove the church van where her grandmother attended church. They said they knew something was wrong when they pulled up and saw the door opened.

Since riding the church van every Wednesday night and Sunday morning, she was always outside ready to get on the bus. She said it was ungodly to be getting ready when you know you should already be ready. Running to get Michael Jr. and rushing out of church she heard the pastor get up and say, "Let's pray for Sister Glenda." But that was all she heard because she was in her car at lightning speed and was headed toward the hospital.

When she got into the emergency room, she was directed to a waiting room to wait. Several of her grandmother's church members were already there including the pastor. That was the first time she had ever saw a Pastor at her home church of Mt. Zion who left his pulpit to be with a member. When she moved back in with her grandmother, Glenda told her grandmother she would be finding her own church and not attending Mt. Zion.

Her grandmother had tried to tell her under the new leadership, Mt. Zion had changed but she did not hear it. She remembered all the strict rules and how you were condemned for this and for that. She had run out of times where she had heard a woman was to submit to her husband. If she did not, she was a sin before God and she would be condemned to hell. She hated looking at the then Rev. William Harper in the pulpit, knowing he would be paying her own momma a visit later that evening. She would often see First Lady Harper staring at her strange during and after service. It was only when she got older, after her mom had died from a car accident at the age of forty, that she learned the true reasons why she was being stared at. Glenda was Rev. Harper's daughter.

Before he was Rev. William Harper, he wanted to marry her mother, but his family told him that she was not good enough for him because she was too dark skinned. Falling to his family demands, he married

Leila Carpenter. She was the total opposite of Glenda's mom's dark mahogany skin tone; she was very fair skinned with soft reddish-brown hair that flowed down her back, thanks to her grandfather who was a white man. Glenda's mom sported an afro but when her hair was straightened, people would tell her she resembled a dark version of Tamara Dobson from *Cleopatra Jones*. The two women were different as night and day but while Leila had his last name, Glenda's mother had his heart. They kept their love affair up until she was ten years old. It was then her mother was tired of being second best and cut things off with her father.

Her mother had met and married a man by the name of Joseph Smith. Joseph was a good man and had made the last twenty years of her life on earth happy. Long gone were the nights when she heard her mother crying when her father left in the middle of the night. All of those days were long gone when Joseph Smith came in. She had never known her mother to laugh as much. When her mother passed, the Harpers conveniently had a family vacation planned on the same week of the funeral. A year later when Glenda had gone to her mother's grave, she saw Rev. Harper there, sobbing at her grave.

When she approached him and he saw her, he stood up and confessed everything to her. She hated Mt. Zion from that moment: The man who stood up in the pulpit and preached and why her grandmother had told her to forgive. It was not until that day in the hospital that she saw the new pastor standing there looking just as concerned as she was that she understood why she needed to forgive. The man who stood before them was not the man who led the church so many years ago that she knew as her father.

The doctor bust through the doors asking for her. She ran to the doctor and the doctor asked her to come with him. One of the church members got Michael Jr. from her, and she ran behind the doctor who told them that her grandmother was not doing well. She had indeed suffered from a massive stroke and the stroke had left her partially paralyzed on her right side and she was barely hanging on. When they got to a closed curtain, the doctor grabbed her hand and told her that he was sorry and to brace herself for what she was about to see.

After several seconds she nodded her head, and the doctor drew back the curtains. Her grandmother looked weak with numerous machines surrounding her beeping. When she walked in, the doctor closed the curtain, walking shakily to the bed, she stood over and smoothed the hair on her head. Her touch caused her grandmother's eyes to flutter opened.

"Baby," her grandmother voice sounded weak.

"No, save your strength," Glenda said, trying to hold back her tears.

"I don't have that much time." Hearing her grandmother say that caused for the tears she was holding back to spring forward as she released a cry from her lips.

"Hush up with all that. You knew I was not going to live forever. I want you to go into my room and look underneath my mattress to find the key for the chest in my closet. In there are all my important papers. You are going to be okay. Do not ever forget, I love you and even in death, you will always feel my love."

Closing her eyes, the monitors started going off and nurses and doctors rushed in to see Glenda crying her eyes out while laying her head on her grandmother's shoulder. They took her pulse and turned off the machines. Just like that her grandmother was gone. After thirty minutes she walked back down the hallway with tears streaming down her face. When she rounded the corner, she saw Richard standing there talking to the other church members and when he saw her, he stopped his conversation and walked directly up to her and grabbed her into his arms. She lost it and he held her until she was able to pull herself together. Richard was a constant fixture at her grandmother's house from that point forward and even after the funeral. Richard had slowly crept into her heart. That was over thirty years ago.

Taking the last few sips of her coffee, she sat her cup down, still watching LaShonda. Glenda knew it was time to share her story with her. She had almost let the rejection from her biological father and how her mother was treated because she was too dark-skinned ruin her chance at true love. Before Richard, Glenda had only dated men that matched her dark skin tone or were darker. Richard was light skinned, some would say high yellow, with an afro of straight black hair that was soft to the touch and the most amazing pair of grey eyes. Even though he had cut his hair to a well-maintained low cut, he still sported waves because of the soft curl pattern that he had. She had rejected Richard so many times and would not even entertain going out with Richard, but one thing Richard was, was consistent. Then finally Richard had had enough and demanded to know why she would not marry him and when she told him the truth, he pulled her in his arms and told her just how magical her dark complexion was and how it had put him under her spell. That she was his black pearl, and he vowed from that moment on to show and treat her just as such from that moment forward. Richard had done just that from that point.

Walking outside into the yard she saw LaShonda sitting with her face to the sky. Walking up to the swing she saw that LaShonda's face still had streaks of tears on it.

"Baby, you, okay?"

Her voice caused LaShonda to jump at the sound of Glenda's question. As she sat up on the swing and looked at Glenda, she released a sigh of relief.

"You cannot be doing that! You know that I am old."

Glenda let out a hmp as she continued to stare at her with that 'Don't try to change the subject look.'

"Yes, I am okay. I was just thinking about some stuff."

Glenda sat down on the swing next to LaShonda, swinging gently with only the silence in the night surrounding them.

"Are you sure? You are not looking right." Glenda immediately placed the back of her hand on her forehead. "You don't feel hot."

"I am fine. I did not take my allergy medicine today and I can tell this grass is freshly cut."

"Yeah, did you bring your medicine? Do you need me to get it?"

"No, I am about to call it a night. I am tired."

"Okay, you know we appreciate you. Thank you for cooking today."

Cooking had always been a passion of LaShonda's. Whenever she got down, she would always find herself in the kitchen trying out a new recipe. By the time she was done, she had normally worked out all her issues or had a good plan in place to conqueror it. She had developed her own recipe for yeast rolls and the Horry Clan had given her the thumbs up. Now for all the family gatherings she made rolls as well as several other dishes.

"Thank you for allowing me."

"Baby do not be too mad at your brothers and sisters. They just want to see you married to someone who will take care of you. You have been hurting for a long time. We all want to see you happy."

"I know, I just wish you all would lay off me and David."

"David is a good man who will make you a good husband."

"Momma Glenda, not right now, okay?"

"Before I go back in, I think I need to share something with you."

"Am I in trouble?" LaShonda asked quickly. She did not recognize the look that was on her face.

"No," Glenda sighed. "But I think it will help you."

"I'm listening."

"When I was eighteen, I got married to Michael West, Michael Jr's father."

"Okay, I know about that."

"Yes, but there are some things I never share outside of when I feel God is leading me to share and tonight, I feel as though it is one of those times."

Swallowing the hard lump that had formed in her throat, LaShonda looked at Momma Glenda and saw the serious look on her face. Shonda did not know what she was about to say but she knew she was about to say something that was going to impact her.

"We were married less than a year when the abuse started. He was abusive... very abusive. He blamed me for everything, and it seemed as though I was the reason behind ALL his failures in life. One day he was reprimanded at work, and he came home mad and drunk. I had just had Michael, and he blamed the fact he was reprimanded because I did not keep the baby quiet enough so he could get a good night's sleep. He beat me that day to the point I had started praying for death. I eventually passed out and when I awoke, I was in the hospital. The beating had caused some tearing and caused me to lose a lot of blood. He eventually had to call the ambulance but left as soon as he did and took my baby with him. The neighbor told them that it was him that had beat me. Michael was later found and arrested."

"I can't believe this," LaShonda said, looking at her with an astonished look on her face. "What happened to Michael Sr.?"

"He went to jail. He was sentenced to twenty years. He had people calling my house threatening me. His family turned their back on me, saying if I were a real woman, I would have known how to take care of my house and not get the police involved. It got so bad I had to move. I moved back to my grandmother's house. Michael was so full of hate and anger. He ended up having a massive heart attack after a while. He never recovered and ended up dying. They called me to let me know because I was still legally married to him."

LaShonda moved closer to her and just hugged her, putting her head on the back of Glenda's shoulder. When she heard Glenda sniffing, she hugged her tighter. She never knew this woman had been through so much. She heard Glenda take a deep breath and felt her patting her arm.

"I showed up at the hospital where they had taken him, and his family was there. As I rounded that corner in the hospital, I immediately felt it; the hate and pure disgust his family had for me. They started shouting and yelling at me, asking me why I was there, that I was the reason he was gone. It was relentless. The police were eventually called, and they were escorted out. I planned the funeral, but I did not go. Even though he was not a good husband, he was a good provider. He had taken out two life insurance policies; one for me and one for Michael Jr. His family fought me on that. They even took me to court to contest the policies. By the time all that was over with Michael Jr. was almost five and I wanted to just give up the money, but my grandmother was not having it. She told me blatantly that, that money he left me was nothing compared to the physical and mental abuse he had put me through."

"I am with Grandma! He should have never put his hands on you but since he did you were due that money," LaShonda responded, sounding angrier than she would like. She could not imagine someone putting their hands on her now. One of them, if not all of them, would be in that person's throat. She knew she had some *Peter's* tendencies and did not hasten to bring it out when necessary and for Momma Glenda, it was not even a second thought. Growing up how she did, she had to learn how to fight and while she did not like to fight, she would go to work to protect those who mattered to her.

"Baby, calm down. I can feel you getting angry," Glenda laughed slightly. Glenda knew LaShonda was very protective and was probably imagining fighting Michael. Glenda pulled LaShonda from behind her to beside her.

"See, when Richard came into my life, he was just a minister. He chased behind me for months; I did not think I was good enough for him."

"I know what that feels like," LaShonda said while looking back up in the sky.

"Baby, I told you that story because I see me in you. I see how David is chasing behind you, and you keep giving him all those excuses. You do not think that you are good enough for him." Glenda watched LaShonda swipe at the tears sprung into her eyes.

"You do not have to tell me, I know. I thought Richard deserved better. However, when I allowed him to really come into my life and let his love really fill those voided areas in my heart, I realized it was *shame* that was telling me I was not good enough. But Richard's love was pure, and it made all those dark areas of heart and pain disappear."

Glenda pulled LaShonda into her arms and she hugged her tightly. "David has a pure love for you. I know you did not tell us everything that Joe did to you. I know it was more than what you told the church but when you are ready to talk, I am here. However, do not allow what Joe did or said to you to make you think that you are not good enough. Because that man in that house has enough love to move all those thoughts out of your life if you allow him to."

Glenda hugged her for a few more minutes. When she felt LaShonda's tears stop, Glenda leaned back and kissed her on the side of her face.

"Allow David to love you and you love him back. You are worthy of true love. Do you believe that?"

Glenda waited until she heard LaShonda answer a faint *yes* that released more sobs. Glenda stood up and watched her for another few moments before answering her own question.

"Yes, you are. It is time for me to go back in. Do not stay out here too long, okay?"

"Yes ma'am."

As she watched Momma Glenda go back in the house, she could feel her heart grow even bigger for that woman. She chuckled as she remembered how it took a long time for her to get used to see how affectionate Bishop Horry and Momma Glenda was to one another. Coming from the dysfunctional family that she grew up in, she was not used to seeing this type of affection between husband and wife. LaShonda had gotten an entirely different viewpoint of what a healthy marriage looked like by watching them.

She had not been prepared when Bishop Horry walked through the door with David on his heels. Bishop Horry went straight to Momma Glenda and kissed her as David paused at the sink, capturing LaShonda's attention immediately.

"So, we meet again. I thought you said you were going home?" David said.

LaShonda looked down at the floor for a couple of moments, wishing the floor could swallow her up. She had forgot the half-truth that she had told David in the parking lot to avoid his attempt to ask her our again.

"This is home, or my second home," she said as she walked past David.

Laughing softly as she recounted the evening's earlier events, LaShonda folded her arms around her as the night temperature began to drop. She felt the scar on her left arm as she did so. The scar came when Joe threw her on the floor, and she hit the corner of one of her end tables. Even though it was healed she could still feel the raised portion on her skin, and it was a constant reminder of what had happened that day.

Until the scar was no longer visible, she vowed to wear long sleeve shirts. Glenda was the first to question her about her attire. Glenda was the first person to wear her arms out and did not care if anyone laughed at her big arms. She kept LaShonda laughing, always saying her fat needed to breathe as much as possible so she would not be sweaty.

LaShonda had never told anyone about what had really happened to Joe. She just told them that they had broken up. When they pressed about why they broke up, her answer was that he did not like the fact that she was in church so much. When she said that, all the ones who were excited about his presence were even more excited about his departure.

She was still upset that she had to spend the money that she had been saving up to get a new laptop on getting all her locks changed and even the counseling that she had undergone to help get past what had happened. She knew she should not let Joe steal any more moments from her, especially when a few weeks after that had happened, she had come home to find him sitting in her driveway.

He thought they could get back together because he was sorry for what he had done. She laughed as she wiped the tears away that had started to fall. She still could not get over the nerve of him.

"That why I left… I knew you were going to try to say I raped you, but you wanted it, and I am a full-grown man. I felt like you were pressuring me into marrying you to get some. I mean I can see if you ain't never had sex before, but it was not your first time."

She remembered Joe's words to her as she repeatedly told him to leave before she called the police. Joe finally left but not before he told her that she was never his main girl. That piece of news nearly destroyed the little bit of dignity that she had. Not only had she opened her heart and her home up to a guy who ended up raping her but to find out she was just the side piece was almost unbearable. Yelling still remembered the mocking look that he gave her as he had pulled out her driveway and then he rolled down the window and threw out the spare key that she had given him, yelling out that she could have it back since it no longer worked before, he sped off.

LaShonda sat back and decided to head back in. It was getting cool, and she needed to get ready to go back in and say her goodbyes. When she came back into the living room the game of Phase 10 had been put to the side and just a good old conversation around the table was being had. Seeing her family sit and laugh made her heart flutter. She was so thankful to have met the Horry's during that time.

"Well, I am sorry to break up the jokes, but I am going to have to call it a night."

After the *awwwww* from them had passed, everyone started to get up and share hugs, signaling that family night had come to an end. As LaShonda put her jacket on and grabbed her purse, she was met by David who told her that he was going to follow her home. Out of the corner of her eye she could see both Michael and Daniel giving him the thumbs up. LaShonda turned around quickly to catch them in the act, but she was not quick enough, since both had put their easily and were acting like they had not done anything.

David walked with her to the car and closed her door. As she backed out, David was right behind her, following her all the way home, and had even gotten out and walked her to her door. As he walked back to his car, she admired the backside that he presented. She knew when she got into the house she would have to repent. She made sure he had gotten into his car; he beeped the horn and sped off before she closed the door.

LaShonda was neither tall nor skinny; in fact, she was medium height and had curves and bumps. She chuckled as she thought about one of the conversations that was held at the dinner table. Kathryn brought up going shopping and Shell busted out and said, "Well, I am just thankful you learned how to dress your fat." David almost choked on the third roll that he had just put in his mouth.

"Shell, I cannot believe you just said that. David, excuse Shell, she does not have any manners." If looks could kill Shell would have been six feet under with the look that Kathryn had given her.

"I am just saying. Shonda, hit the line for her." Shell turned and looked at LaShonda, knowing that she was about to drop her famous words of wisdom that she gave to all plus sized women when going shopping.

"Back fat is real and when you are no longer in denial about it, you can do something about it," LaShonda proclaimed with a grin.

The table erupted in laughter. LaShonda was sitting right next to David when he laughed, and their hands touched slightly. When their gazes met, she quickly diverted her eyes from his. The heat she felt from him made her quickly pull her hand back. David was so handsome to her. He had immaculately kept locs that hung down his back with his deep caramel skin color and slight build; he was not fit but he was not disproportionate either. And judging by how he had eaten at dinner, she knew he liked to eat but also knew he was a regular jogger due to on some Sundays, he changed into his workout clothes prior to leaving the church. Trina's voice interrupted the laughter.

"Well, everyone can't be a size 1!"

"Well, everyone does not like one. Some people like 8s, 9s, 10s, 22s." David said as Michael wrapped him up.

"Thank God for our daddy who taught us to appreciate all women because we don't know how God will wrap the gift of the Lord up!" Michael said as David stood up and started acting like he was about to preach.

"Well, Wellllll!" sang Daniel in the corner, encouraging David to continue.

"But we just got to be ready, ready, ReeeeeeeeaDY! To unwrap the gift. Your gift might come being 5'5" and slim or in the words of a good brethren… slim, thick… you just got to be Ready! To unwrap the gift. Because it is going to bring joy, unspeakable joy, to you and your soul. For when you get the blessing of the Lord, it will bring you peace and riches like no other. She will bless you and everything around you. For she will be your favor!"

Michael stood up and shouted, "You better Preach!" He sat back down, grabbed Denise's hand, and kissed the back of it, causing a faint blush to gradually spread across her face.

"Preach, preacher," Daniel said, taking out his wallet, and getting a dollar, and putting it in front of David.

"I'm about to pass the mic, pass the mic because you all are being cheap." David picked up the dollar and put it in his jacket. "But we are going to praise the Lord for it. Anyway, Brother Michael, take it from here."

Michael stood up and pushed his glasses up in his face.

"So, you see, Thank you, Brother Sanders. I want you to know that God is saying in this hour, you got to be ready. Ready for his blessing, for some blessings will only come through a window while others may come through the door. You may be wondering what I am talking about. I am saying some blessing you will see while looking out the window and some you will see while walking through some doors, but you just got to be ready!!! For when and how the blessing will cross your path. Brother Daniel, do you have anything to say on this matter?"

Jumping up and grabbing the wooden spoon,

"I think everything that needs to be said has been said," Daniel said as he stood up.

"Now, as we come to a close, I feel as though we all are ready. Ready to eat, I feel in my sanctified soul that some desserts are around the corner. My nostrils had not failed me yet and the tingling smells of..." Daniel sniffed the air, "Peach cobbler," sniffed the air again, "Banana pudding, and I think maybe even some ice cream is awaiting us. Can I get Amen?"

Glenda, who had been laughing the entire time, grabbed a towel and threw it at Daniel.

"Boy, you know you ain't smelling no ice cream from the deep freezer." She dabbed.

her eyes with a napkin as she laughed.

"Okay ladies let us get dessert ready. Men, clean the table."

Glenda led the herd of women to the kitchen as the men continued to preach the message.

Chapter 6

LaShonda came out of the bathroom with her night clothes on and climbed into her bed to lay back on to the pile of pillows. She shook her head in memory of the men and their so-called sermon. She would love more than anything to date David, but she just did not think it was possible. David came from a well-to-do family, and she did not even know who her real parents were. She had been left at the hospital. That was all she knew. For all she knew she walked past her mother every day.

She rolled over onto her side as her tears started to fall. Everyone thought that she was just being mean or did not know that David liked her, but that was not the case. She was quite aware of David's feelings, and the sad thing was that he invaded her dreams many nights and daily daydreams. She really did like David, but she knew David deserved better. She was recycled goods, and no one would want her if they knew the truth about how she had been raped and molested repeatedly growing up or the truth about how her nasty uncle, who thought just because she wasn't blood, that it was ok to make her do adult things.

She remembered how Uncle Edward would be so mean to her in public, calling her names, throwing things at her, and just doing about anything to make sure she knew that she did not belong to their family. Maybe it was his justification that he needed to make him think it was okay to do the things he did to her and the things he made her do to him. *Blood was thicker than water* was what she was always taught.

David did not deserve someone like her. Someone that had been *used*. Yes, she and David could only be together in her fantasy. David's parents had come to visit church not too long after he had joined. David was a PK; his father was a well-known Bishop in the Atlanta area, but he did not believe in holding his children back. When David said he was led to move to South Carolina, his father was in full support.

David had testified many times how God had led him to this city and to the church one Saturday night. He was just driving around exploring the city and he turned on to the road of the church which was blocked off. There he saw kids running around with water guns and huge slip and slides were everywhere. It was the annual Beat the Heat Water Party for the community.

Thinking he was a volunteer from the community, a woman threw him a shirt and told him to come on.

When he was helping them clean up at the end of the event, a group of organizers came to him, thanking him for his help and letting him know that all the volunteers were being invited out to dinner as a thank you. Once again, he got in the car and followed them to the restaurant.

That evening, he laughed and joked around with the crew and on that Sunday, he went back to the church and joined. They were so excited to have him join when he gave his testimony about how he was just driving by and stopped to see what was going on. He talked about standing there and looking around and suddenly, a shirt was thrown at him. Having played both high school and college football, he easily caught the shirt and followed the woman. When Bishop Horry asked who it was that did it, he pointed directly at LaShonda.

Laughing, she remembered how she was so embarrassed, she wanted to die just for a little while, and her face showed it. The entire church was laughing as Bishop Horry started coughing, as tears streamed down his face from laughing. LaShonda was called to come from the minister section so David and she could be formally introduced. LaShonda muttered a soft apology to him and David grabbed her and pulled her into his embrace, telling her no apology was needed.

He had no doubt that moment led him to where he was supposed to be.

His dad had approved his choice of worship after visiting. When they found out through his father that he could sing, David was asked to lead a song. He got up and lead praise and worship on one Sunday. God moved so mightily in that service that he was soon asked to serve as praise and worship leader right then. The previous praise and worship leader had just left the church, stating that he had felt led to open his own church. Bishop Horry always said to not worry about who walked away because if there were a void anywhere God would fill it because He was not about leaving anything undone. That was almost eight years ago.

LaShonda grabbed the pillow and squeezed it tight. Eight symbolized the year of new beginning. She remembered the day that he had joined the church and had whispered that in her ear. It was as though she heard the Holy Spirit tell her that *he would be an immense help to her*, and he had been. She and David had worked on several projects together and he was even over the music ministry. He was also a huge help in planning the Youth Conferences and activities. Yes, David had been an immense help to her, but she needed sleep to find her so that she could dream of a reality her present state could only hope for.

As she closed her eyes, she began to recite the confession that she knew by heart.

"You will give your beloved sleep and because I am your beloved that promise is for me. That it will be sweet sleep." LaShonda started to feel the stress and pain leave her as her eyes started to close. "Lord, I thank you for keeping your promise to me for sweet sleep."

And with that, she closed her eyes and was out for the night.

Chapter 7

It was the third Friday of the month and LaShonda was rushing to get home so she could get to Casey's house. Each month, the singles at their church got together for fellowship. For this month they decided to meet at Casey's house and next month would be at LaShonda's. She had promised Casey she would get there early and help with setting up everything. Whoever hosted the event had to produce the debate question of the night and some activities for everyone. Even though it was supposed to be Casey's turn, she felt like it was hers, too.

Using her spare key to Casey's house, LaShonda came in with a hand full of bags and saw Casey in the living room vacuuming.

"Girl, let me help you," Casey said, dropping the vacuum to grab some of the bags out of her hands.

"I cannot thank you enough for helping me. School and work are kicking my tail."

"No problem, girl. You know I got your back." LaShonda closed the door with her foot and rushed toward Casey upon seeing Casey putting the bags down one by one.

"Aht, aht! Put those bags down!"

Protesting with a pout, Casey put her hands on her hips, "But I'm hungry!"

"You will eat when everyone else eats," LaShonda said, eyeing Casey.

"You're mean." Casey said as she moved to the table to start taking packages out of the bags.

"And you are a mess," LaShonda said as she placed a tray of sandwiches near her to keep.

it in her sight. She had ordered a sandwich tray from Casey's favorite sandwich shop as a surprise, and she knew she should have gone with her first thought, which was to leave them in the car until it was time for them to be served.

They had been working for almost an hour and the house was almost ready for visitors.

She had brought the ingredients to make her meatballs and cheese dip to accompany the other items. Because many of the singles at the church were single parents, they provided foods for their events and planned an activity for both the children and the adults. This month, Casey had asked LaShonda to speak to the adults. They were in her activity room setting up the games for the children when the doorbell rang.

"Who could that be? It is still early," LaShonda asked, glancing at her watch to see it was only 6:55 pm. Most of the members never arrived prior to 7:45 pm.

"I don't know, but can you answer the door for me?" Casey asked as she set up the large Jenga blocks.

LaShonda moved to the door, looked through the peep hole, and saw David. She let out a long breath, putting her head on the door. Of course, it was him. Gaining her composure, she opened the door.

"Hey, David. You are early?"

"Hey, Shonda. Yeah, Casey had asked me to get here early to help with set up."

"Okay, well, we are in here setting up the kids' zone." LaShonda noticed that he had bags, so she reached for them.

"Here, let me get these."

"Thanks. It is different desserts in there."

LaShonda took the bags and sat them on the dessert table. David had brought an assortment of miniature cakes, sugar cookies, and chocolate covered pretzels. She tried to inconspicuously hide two sugar cookies away while she was setting out the desserts. Those were her absolute favorite but when she heard Casey's clear her throat, she knew she had been caught. Turning around she was not going down without a fight and a cookie.

"Everything is okay," LaShonda said, trying to look as innocent as she could.

"Put the cookies back. I saw you. If I cannot have a sandwich before, you cannot have a cookie either," Casey said, holding out her hand.

"See, there is the difference between me and you. I am going to eat mine later. I just sat it to the side so I can ensure I get one."

Rolling her eyes, Casey turned to go to the kitchen. "You get on my nerves. I am about to check on the food in the kitchen. I will be right back."

Casey had disappeared towards the kitchen before David spoke.

"You two are crazy. Is there anything with which I can help?"

"Yes, come on."

The trio traded idle chit chat while they made sure everything was set and ready to go by the time the doorbell rung with the first guest. It was the usual crowd, but they had a new guest also. One of the newest members, Darlene, had just joined the group. Darlene was a little older, but you could tell that she was on edge all the times. She had joined the church over a year ago and she was finally getting to the point of joining in on some of the activities.

"Okay, I want to thank you all for attending this month's Singles Mixer. Now that the children are in their own world, it is time for us to get to the activity of the night. I asked Shonda to speak tonight so let us give our undivided attention to her," Casey started once everyone had settled. LaShonda stood in front of

Casey's fireplace before the adults seated at tables in a U-shape.

"Hello, I hope you all have enjoyed the food and talk so far. Tonight, I am going to start off with an activity and I need a volunteer." Alicia raised her hand and went to the front. Once Alicia arrived, LaShonda proceeded to bring out a blindfold.

"Okay, as you all know, what goes on in here, stays in this room. This is a safe environment, okay?"

LaShonda watched as everyone nodded in agreement before pulling out two crisp bills: one $50 and the other $100. She told Alicia the money was hers if she could find it while blindfolded. Once Alicia agreed, LaShonda blindfolded her and then placed the money by the sofa. However, she gave several people notes to yell directions that would lead her away *from* the pot while Shonda gave directions that would lead her *to* the pot.

"Okay, Alicia, I have placed the money so now I want you to listen to me in order to get to the pot." LaShonda proceeded to start telling her how to go forward and as she did, others started yelling in other directions. Soon, Alicia was almost in the children's room before LaShonda stopped her and told her she was lost. Alicia took off the blindfold and she saw how far she was from the prize.

LaShonda looked disappointed as she asked Alicia why she did not follow the directions that she was giving. It was there that Alicia said that she did not fully trust LaShonda because she did not know her and that she was so in tune with trying to listen voices she thought she could trust. LaShonda thanked Alicia for volunteering and for her honesty as she placed the money back in her pocket and started her lesson.

"In life, this is what happens when we do not spend time with God, and we are going through it. We miss God because we are too busy trying to pay attention to voices that we think we can trust and then we end up so far off the mark that we sometimes miss our blessings. See, I had the money but because Alicia did not trust me, she could not get into it. She trusted people who she thought knew the process or the journey, causing her to get off course from what God had her on."

"This going to be good." Cheryl said as she high fived the girl next to her.

"See, God has a plan for all of us, however, as life happens, we allow other people and other voices to become louder than God and God cannot lead you when He is not allowed to. You too busy looking at man instead of God, and when you get in a situation outside of God, we want to blame God. We want to ask God *why*, but it is not God's fault that you allowed someone else voice to be louder than His in your life. You must take the blame for that and take responsibility to get back on course. Not one time did Alicia yell out to me for help because she did not trust me. But when she saw she was so far off, she knew then those other voices were leading her astray but the one she should have trusted, she ignored."

"Lord, are your feet hurting?" David said, looking at Casey.

"Are they!" Casey was looking exasperated.

"God will never fail us; HE will retest us and many of us are single now, some by choice and for some, the choice was made for us. Whether or not it was because they broke up with us or walked out on us, we are single. I am fairly sure that many of us thought that we would be married by now. Honestly, I never thought about marriage. I had such low self-esteem; my goal was a live-in boyfriend and a double wide." The room erupted with laughter. "You all are laughing but it is true. I was left with DSS at eighteen months, my foster family was abusive and not all of it was just physical abuse; some of it was sexual."

The room grew quiet, and more people waited for the next word that came out of her mouth. She knew she had grabbed their attention, especially with what she was feeling led to share with them. She had called the Byrds who were over the Singles Ministry and told them what she felt like God was leading her to share. They told her to do what God had told her to do. Looking over to see them, both were nodding their heads, encouraging her to continue.

"See, when I was eight, I found myself in the backroom with a nasty uncle." The room gasped; she saw tears forming in some of their eyes. Being black and being a woman in America unfortunately made you more prone to have been sexual assaulted by a family member. She knew that several women in that room had been assaulted and she prayed that what she was about to share would set some of them free from the shame that she had felt for so long.

"For years, this happened and when I was fifteen, I found myself pregnant." Tears that she had held back for so long started to form but she did not allow them to fall yet – she needed to finish this.

"Fifteen and pregnant and my uncle was my baby's father. My foster mother got so angry when I tried to tell her it was her brother that she beat me. I mean, she jumped on me and beat me. I was fifteen fighting a grown woman. That next morning, I woke up at 2:33 am with sharp pains and I had a miscarriage. I remember she looked at me, called me trash, and told me that I lost my baby because it was a bastard just like me."

Sniffles could be heard by some of the members. Casey walked around with the tissue box as LaShonda continued.

"For a long time, I thought I should just settle for anything that came my way and just like those other voices that Alicia listened to, they got me away from the Will of God in *my life*. I settled and those settlements landed me in a lot of abusive and narcissist relationships.

I thought I did not deserve someone who would love me unconditionally and that type of love was for others and not myself. Many of you know I had a young man accompanying me last year to the church and some of you in this room told me how I looked so happy and how cute we were." LaShonda sighed, and turning around, she prayed for strength before finally taking her power back from the shame that had held her captive for the last year.

"What you all do not know is that he was a narcissist. Everything that went wrong in his life was *my fault*, and he would say the meanest things to me. And when I finally got enough and tried to break up with him, he beat me." Lashonda could hear some in the room sniffling as she paused to allow the depths of what she had just said to sink in before she continued.

"He bruised my arm and my forehead and when he wanted to drive his point across, he hit me so hard, I stumbled to the floor. He then held me down and raped me in my own house." The tears that she had been holding back started to fall but her voice was surprisingly still strong. She knew it was God. "I was so ashamed. I beat myself up for getting raped but through therapy and God, I know that I *did not* deserve this. And I know that God is leading me to share this tonight because it is someone else in here dealing with the Spirit of Shame. It is not your fault for dealing with sick individuals. You could not have dressed or acted any differently because regardless, they had made up in their hearts and minds to do that to you. The enemy wants you to be ashamed like it is your fault to the point that some of you even still think it is your job to protect your family from the truth. But if it hurt you, it is time to deal with it."

Darlene started to wail, along with several other women. Casey had gone to sit with the children and closed the door to keep them occupied. The one that surprised everyone was her sister, Trina. She was on the floor bawling. Everyone came around and prayer took place, and the Spirit of Shame was being cast out of all the members that came up for prayer. As the tears slowed, Elder Byrd got up and asked if anyone else wanted to get up and share their testimony and Darlene volunteered.

Darlene got up and started talking about how she was an abused woman. She finally got the strength and courage to leave. She had found a job, but her ex-boyfriend kept showing up and she had just lost her job. She was about to lose everything and was about to end her life when David called her and reminded her of the meeting. Turning and looking at David, she said, "I just want to say thank you for making me agree to come tonight. I did not want to break my word to you and now I know it was meant for me not to miss this meeting tonight. God is not done with me, and I just need to hold on." When Darlene sat down in her seat, Melissa placed her arms around her and hugged her.

"Girl, let us love on you. Then give us your number. We are family and we look out for each other. Just five years ago, my husband left me for another woman, and I thought that was it and wanted to end my life. I felt so ugly and ashamed, but this group right here is what loved me back to life and now it is your turn," Melissa said as she embraced Darlene. The love that Darlene started to feel made her start laughing and crying at the same time.

Everyone was sitting around talking among themselves when Trina stood up and cleared her throat.

"I want to thank you, Shonda, for sharing that. I know everyone knows that Shonda is not my blood sister, but I will fight you if you mess with her as if she was. I was crying for two reasons tonight. One, I knew something had happened with her and I am so thankful she walked through it and is now helping others. And the second reason is, I was raped three years ago on my way home from class one night. I was so ashamed and that is why I started acting out and dressing crazy. I mean, I was the Pastor's daughter. I should have known how to discern spirits, but I thought we were just having a study date, and he raped me in the back part of the library. Then he told me to hurry up and get dressed before we got caught. He acted like he did not hear me say *no*."

LaShonda went up and wrapped her arms around her sister and just as Glenda had done, rocked her until she felt peace enter Trina's body as she silently thank God for allowing her to share her testimony about what she had gone through. What the enemy meant for evil God was working it out for her good.

❁

❧ LATER THAT EVENING

That evening continued well into the night. It was after midnight before everyone left Casey's house. Once

Trina shared, some of the men even started getting up and sharing them experience of being sexually abused. LaShonda had brought a bag to sleep over at Casey's just in case it got too late. David had hung around to help clean up and put her house back together and also helped to pray over Casey's house for her home to be purified after all that healing. LaShonda was standing in Casey's den where the kids had been, and she had just put the last toy up when she felt a presence in the room with her. She turned to see David.

"Shonda, I tell you. You are amazing."

"No," she replied, shaking her head. "It is all God."

"Well, God needed a vessel, and can you accept the fact that I want to thank you for being that vessel tonight?" David held her gaze until she finally smiled.

"Thank you, David."

"You're welcome, Shonda. Can I ask you a question?" "Yes."

"Is that the reason you didn't want to date me?" "Didn't?"

"Yes, did not. I mean, after tonight, you said that Spirit of Shame is no longer on you." "David…"

"Shonda, when I joined the church, I heard God say that you would be an immense help to me."

"What?" LaShonda gasped, looking at him with an incredulous look on her face. "Yes, and Shonda, I have been patience with you, but I want to take this, take *us*, to another level."

Turning around she bowed her head. Tears started to fall.

"Yes, it was th reason why I didn't want to date you, David." Lashonda said while her head looking towards the floor.

"So, does that mean we can now explore this attraction between us? I mean, we can take it slow, but I want you to know that what he tried to do…" David covered the distance between them in two strides, grabbing LaShonda's hand and slowly turning her to face him.

"… did not work. I still see you as a virtuous and righteous woman that I would proudly parade around as my woman. So, Shonda, can we?"

Trying to hold back more tears, LaShonda slowly nodded her head *yes*. As David pulled her into his arms and hugged her, she felt as if she was releasing all the pressure that she had held her for so long and while it was heavy, he was built to handle it.

Chapter 8

❧ SIX MONTHS LATER

L ast night, LaShonda and David celebrated their six-month anniversary. He had taken her out to her favorite restaurant and had invited their entire clan. While many speculated that he was going to propose, he did not, and it was just a nice dinner. In a few months it would be her birthday, and she was planning a huge fortieth birthday party so she assumed he would do it then instead. She had taken today off just to rest, knowing that she would probably be tired later today. People thought she was disappointed because he did not propose but she was not, in fact, she was relieved. She did not know if she was ready for such a step yet.

Waking up to a sun filled room, she felt good about having the ability to sleep in today. Looking towards the clock, she knew it was at least ten in the morning; however, when she looked, it was only 7:20 am.

"My body betrays me once again! It is our day off, why are you waking up like we have to go to work?" LaShonda laid back down even though she knew that sleep would not find her. She had always been an early riser since she was young. Staying at her foster family's house, she never slept in. It was always her job to get up and start cleaning and even cooking breakfast if necessary. Shaking her head, with one hand, she tossed the covers off her and proceeded to get out of the bed when her phone started vibrating. Glancing at the clock in her dresser she knew it was her *good morning* text from David. Picking up her phone, she knew she looked silly smiling all big and she had not even read the first words of the text.

7:23 am - David

Good morning, Sunshine. I hope you have a beautiful day today. May it be as sunny as my day is with thoughts of you. Love You. Enjoy your day off.

7:28 am - Shonda

Good morning, handsome. My day is always great when I see your name scroll across my phone. You have the ability to make my cloudy days seem bright. Thank you for a wonderful evening last night. Cannot wait to see you tomorrow. Talk to you later, My Love

LaShonda fell back on to the bed and started to laugh. David had given her the ability to be herself comfortably. At first, she was shy and did not know how to really take David. She did not want to give him any pet names because of fearful reminders of how her ex hated pet names. David loved it and had given her the nickname Sunshine.

7:35 am - David

Excuse the delay. I had to squeeze my head into the door this morning. You got me sprung. If I were a genie, you would be the only one that I would want to grant wishes for. About to clock in. I love you. Will call you at lunch.

7:37 am - Shonda

♥

She responded with a simple heart. She laid her phone down and closed her eyes and yelled, "Thank you God!" David had definitely been an added blessing to her life. She jumped out of bed, saying her key word to turn on her Mimi app that turned her light on in her bedroom, and started playing her favorite radio station as she headed to the bathroom. She did a full body stretch in front of the mirror and was astonished to see a large blood stain on her t-shirt. Immediately, the alarms in her head started going off.

She knew it was blood. She tried not to panic as she started trying to see if there were any cuts on her body. She knew her bed was crowded with stuff. Because she was not a wild sleeper, she often had one side of her bed filled with notebooks, books, crafting material, etc. After taking off her shirt and doing an examination of the area where the spot was located, she did not see any cuts on her stomach.

"You know what, I wonder if I had spilled something on it and did not know. I mean, I did not see any blood on my bedding this morning," she said aloud, trying to reassure herself.

Letting out a long sigh, she headed out of her bathroom and went to her bed where she grabbed up the pillow she went to sleep holding. She saw the same spot on the other side. When she snatched the pillowcase off, she saw it had bled onto the pillow and the sheet. She pulled the sheet back and saw it was another stain on her pillow top mattress.

"Okay, Shonda, do not panic. We need to see where this blood is coming from."

Going back into the bathroom, she put the shirt back on. Angling her body in the mirror to see the side where the blood was located, she smoothed the shirt down and saw that the spot was directly under her left breast. Stunned and confused, she knew blood was not supposed to come out of her breast. Taking the shirt off again, she lifted her breast up. She was turning forty this year and with her being heavy chested, her breasts' perky days were behind her. As she examined the breast, she did not see any bloody spots.

"Okay, Shonda, get it together. It is no way that your breast is leaking blood." She was trying to say something to lessen the anxiety that she had started feeling. She gave her breast a little squeeze and with just that little squeeze, she saw blood coming from her nipple. She grabbed a tissue and wiped the blood away. Going back to her bed, she grabbed her phone and called Casey. Casey was her RN and future FNP friend. LaShonda looked at the clock, knowing that she would be on her way to work. Casey noticed the second ring.

"Good morning, friend!" Casey's peppy voice came through the phone.

"Good morning, girl. How are you?"

"I am good; excited that today is my final night in class. I will be scheduling for my FNP examination soon."

LaShonda started to scream through the phone.

"I am so proud of you! Girl, I cannot wait! And you know the turn up is going to be real."

Casey laughed. "Yes, this is our degree. All those nights I wanted to quit, and you would not let me do that. You kept pushing me and would not let me settle. I am so thankful for a friend like you. I love you girl, and I really mean it."

Both women started laughing at the inside joke that they shared. One day when Casey and LaShonda first started being good friends, Casey was going through something with her then - boyfriend Miles. LaShonda helped her get through that point and when she was walking through the door she turned and said, ' 'I love you."

Casey was on the verge of saying it when LaShonda cut her off and said, ' 'I do not mean it." After Casey called her all kinds of crazy, they both laughed and that had been the foundation of their friendship.

"Girl, you would have done the same for me. You know you my Sista!" "You know it! So how are you going to spend your off day today?"

LaShonda paused.

"I don't know but I called because I got a question for you."

"Ok, what's up?" Casey asked inquisitively.

"So, you know with us reaching forty, our body be doing different things, right?"

"Girl, what done happened, so we can add it to our list?" Casey and both LaShonda shared a laugh. With Casey about to turn forty-four and LaShonda about to turn forty, they had started a list of what to expect when turning forty that they would share at LaShonda's fortieth birthday party.

LaShonda knew she could not just laugh this away. She took a deep breath before she said aloud what had just happened.

"My nipple is leaking blood."

Casey, who was still laughing, immediately stopped and became alarmed. "Blood... Blood? That ain't supposed to happen. Have you contacted your doctor?"

"No, it just happened." LaShonda said in a calming voice, trying to signal Casey to also be calm but Casey was not hearing none of that.

"Girl, call your doctor right now and get an appointment."

"It is not that serious. I mean, I am not in any pain. It is just leaking a little when I squeeze it."

"Girl do not make me call Momma Glenda on you! I better be hearing by the time I get to this office that you have contacted your doctor. If I do not, please know I am calling Momma Glenda." Silence met Casey from the other end.

"Shonda, do I make myself clear?"

"Yes, Mother!" LaShonda said sarcastically.

"Do not you play with me, ma'am. Get on that phone now." Casey abruptly hung up the phone.

Rolling her eyes to the heavens, LaShonda knew that she should not have called her. Picking up the phone, she scrolled for the number to her gynecologist.

She immediately liked Dr. Krystal Johnson when she met her a few years ago. Instead of calling, she made the decision to send an email through the patient portal. It was her first day off in months and she really did not want to go to the doctor for something that she thought might be insignificant.

✻

Hi, Dr. Johnson,

I hope all is well. This morning, I woke up to my left breast leaking blood. It was a good amount. It bled through my shirt, but I am OK and I am not in any pain. It is still leaking a little bit but again, I am not in any pain. Please let me know what I should do next.

LaShonda

✻

Hitting the send button, LaShonda felt confident that it was nothing. She made sure to emphasize that she was not in any pain. She had started cleaning when she heard her phone ring. She looked at the clock to see it was 8:15 am and figured it was Casey making good on her threat. Before she could say hello, Casey's voice came through the phone.

"Did you call?"

"I sent an email."

"Really, Shonda? An email! I am about to come and bust you up."

"Look, she will read it and get back in touch with me if she thinks it's anything."

"I am so done with you. You get on my last nerve! I will call back in a few to see if she has responded."

The call ended abruptly again, and she knew Casey was spitting fire mad with her. She knew Casey loved her, but she could be a little overbearing at times. She thought that she knew what was best for LaShonda all the time. Many did not understand that because she had basically raised herself from the age of ten, she had become self-sufficient and at times, she could do without the constant accusations like she was a child. That got on LaShonda's nerves to no ends at times.

While Casey had family that she could rely on throughout her life, that had not been LaShonda's story. She remembered her foster mother coming to her on her fifteenth birthday and telling her to get a job and pay rent or get out. Not knowing that her foster mom was getting a check for her, she went looking for a job. She knew her foster mother's other older kids, who were her own biological children, did not have to pay rent and it did not seem fair that she had to.

When she asked her foster mom, it was a simple answer for her, "They are blood." LaShonda finally found a job at a local fast-food restaurant where she quickly moved up the chain. Her foster mother made her pay her $300 a month for rent and made her buy groceries once a month. LaShonda could not think of a time when she did not have to take care of herself. Sighing, she went into the kitchen to get some items to clean the blood stain from her mattress.

LaShonda was furiously scrubbing her mattress clean when her phone rang.

"Hello, Ms. Barnes. This is Molly with Dr. Johnson's office. I was calling you about your inquiry through the patient portal."

"Okay."

"Dr. Johnson wants you to go for a mammogram as soon as possible."

"A mammogram? I am not even forty yet and my insurance is not going to pay for it," LaShonda argued, trying to make sure she did not spill the water onto the mattress.

"This will be a diagnostic test and not a screening. Your insurance will pay for a diagnostic before forty. Is there a particular imaging place you would like to be scheduled at?"

"Ummm, I do not know. I never had one."

"OK, I am going to do some calling to try to get you in some place today. I will be calling you back in a few."

"Okay."

Molly hung up the phone and LaShonda looked down at her shirt. She had put on a clean shirt and no blood was on it. She was hoping that it was just something that had randomly happened and would not happen again. Breathing deeply, she took off the shirt off and placed both hands to cup her left breast. She squeezed and once again blood started oozing out of the nipple.

As tears rolled down her face, LaShonda cried, "Lord, what is going on with my body?"

Chapter 9

Molly had called back and told her that she had to be downtown in an hour at the Imaging Center. Sitting in the waiting room with all the pink ribbon that surrounded her, fear leaped into her heart. She was scared. *Lord, what if it is cancer?* Trying not to let the fear of cancer leap into her head because she was a woman of faith, she settled her current medical issue being something like a blood vessel or something that was causing the bloody discharge from her breast.

Looking around the office she saw people patiently sitting in the waiting room.

This did not feel real. How did a nice relaxing day at the house turn into an emergency mammogram? She had called Momma Glenda to tell her that she was on her way to a mammogram screening. She tried to be as evasive as possible, but Momma Glenda was not having it. ' 'So, what is going on with your breasts?" was her first question. After explaining what happened, Glenda sighed, said a quick prayer, and told her to give her a call once she came from the office. She and Bishop Horry were on the way to a funeral.

"Ms. Barnes?" A nurse tech came around the corner interrupting her thoughts.

"Yes, that's me." LaShonda followed behind the nurse tech as they entered what was labeled the Pink Hallway. A lump formed in her throat.

"Ms. Barnes. Ms. Barnes?"

"I'm sorry, what did you say…" looking at the nurse's name tag, "Sara?"

"I said we will be leaving you here for a few moments and then someone else or myself will come get you when we have a room available."

"Thank you," LaShonda said.

She walked into the second waiting room and took a seat, idly playing games on her phones for almost an hour before Sara came back to get her.

"We apologize for the wait, but they did tell you that we were working you in today, right?"

"Yes, they did, and I am off today so I am fine." LaShonda assured her, giving the nurse a smile.

"Well, we have a room ready for you if you will follow me."

LaShonda followed the nurse a few turns before they entered a room with a small bench built into the wall with another door that led into the mammogram room. Sara went into that room and came back with a pink bag with a gown.

"Ok, you are going to put this gown on, and you can place your things in here. Depending on what is seen on the mammogram they may have to do an ultrasound."

"An ultrasound?" Before Shonda could ask, Sara was gone again.

Doing as she was instructed; she took off her shirt and bra and put the gown on. She had just placed everything in the bag when Sara came back in.

"Ok, we are ready for you." She had heard many women talked about this experience with having their breasts mashed but she never thought she would be doing this before the age of forty. Sara quickly had her standing in various positions, getting different angles of her breast. Soon as that was over, she was led back into the first area. Picking up her phone, she realized she needed a distraction before her nerves got the best of her. After what seemed like an eternity, which was only three rounds of Toon Blasts, the door opened, and Sara came in with a new nurse.

Sara looked at her apologetically and informed LaShonda that the mammogram had shown a few areas of concerns, and she would need an ultrasound, and that Jan would be her ultrasound tech. Jan greeted her before requesting that she get her stuff and follow her. LaShonda found herself following another nurse down another hallway covered in pink with pictures. Once being led into the room; she was told to remove her gown and lay on the table. As she laid on the table the nurse tech put some gel on her left breast. As she began to scan over her breast, she made idle chit chat until she saw something that made her facial expression change. Looking at the screen, LaShonda knew it was shocking news before the tech said anything. She knew the techs were not allowed to discuss the imaging, but her breath caught in her throat as she saw the large white spot on the screen.

Tears immediately formed in her eyes. Before getting into the social work field, Shonda had worked in the medical field throughout school to make money. She had worked in Medical Records as a Medical Biller. Having read much medical history and diagnosis she had acquired a few skills that helped her even today. She had become adept at reading radiology reports. She could recall being on call during some weekends when she had to meet the police at the hospital to deal with physically and sometimes sexually abused children. There was nothing more heartbreaking than a young girl turning her head in shame due to the rape kit examination. She had wiped many tears and held many hands. Now lying on this table looking at what she was looking at, she wished someone were there to hold her own hand. She knew that what she was looking at was not good.

When Jan looked down after hearing the sniffle that escaped through LaShonda's lips, she tried to give her a reassuring smile. "Well, they said three areas and

I am only seeing one. Let me get the doctor so he can take a look."

As Jan left the room, LaShonda's eyes became transfixed on the image that was on the screen. The white spot seemed larger than life. Within a few minutes a doctor accompanied Jan back into the room.

"Hello, I am Dr. Michaels, let me take a look at something right quick." Dr. Michaels immediately came into the room and washed his hands after introducing himself. Picking up the scanner he began to inspect the area that Jan had previously done on the ultrasound. He watched the screen as he moved the scanner smoothly across her breast due to the gel. He then started pushing into the breast.

Looking down at her, Dr. Michaels gave her an apologetic look.

"Sorry. I am trying to get a better image. Just a few more moments, okay?" Not waiting for an answer, he continued to scan and push in certain areas.

After several moments of silence and just an occasional "un huh" from Dr. Michaels, he turned and looked at Jan before saying, "Ok, you have been redeemed. It is only two spots."

Turning the machine off, Dr. Michaels requested that LaShonda sit up. Doing a quick breast examination, he stepped back and went to wash his hands again. As Dr. Michaels sat down in the rolling chair, LaShonda knew what he was about to say was about to change her life as she knew it.

"Ms. Barnes, you have two spots that concern us. It shows us some calcifications and to determine if they are cancerous or not, we will need to do a biopsy on both of those sites."

Shocked, LaShonda started to stutter, "You are saying I may have cancer?"

"It is a possibility but the quickest way to determine is to get you biopsied as soon as possible. Do you have a history of breast cancer in your family?"

"I do not know. I grew up in foster care."

"With your age and you not knowing any of your family history, we cannot rule out anything. Jan is going to get you scheduled for your biopsy. We are going to take good care of you, ok?"

Jan was already on the other computer looking at schedules as Dr. Michaels exited the room. It was decided that LaShonda would get the procedure done in two weeks. She knew she needed that time to comprehend what was going on. Things had moved entirely too fast, and she could not believe she was walking out of the office with a pink bag. She got in her car in the parking garage, buckled her seatbelt, and started her car but found herself unable to move. Sitting in the car alone, she finally allowed herself to do the one thing she had been trying not to do all day... sobbed her heart out.

Chapter 10

❧ 2 WEEKS AND 2 DAYS LATER

LaShonda nervously kept glancing at her phone. The anxiety that she had experienced in the last two weeks had been nerve wrecking. She had her biopsy on her left breast done on that Friday and they had told her that they would call her on Monday with the results. It was 7:57 a.m. and David had already texted her good morning, but she had not been able to respond to him. She felt awful for canceling on him in the last couple of weeks and making up excuses about why she could not go out. But her mind was consumed with her possible diagnosis. She just needed to get her negative report and then she would tell him. Momma Glenda tried to get her to tell him, but she could not. Glancing down at her phone again, she knew they could be calling any moment now.

"Girl, get a grip," she said to herself.

The doctor's office was not even open yet. LaShonda had barely gotten any sleep, and she was ready to get her results back that showed that the tumor was non-cancerous, and no further action would need to be taken. It was all the news that she needed. She had already planned to take Friday off just to relax and thank God for allowing all her paperwork to come back in negative. The Sunday before when she went to church, she had gone and gave God some extra praise. Her pastor and friends had all touched and agreed that the finding was nothing. Even though her faith was there, the human side of her was weak. For the last two weeks she had barely slept without the aid of some type of sleep medicine and even with that, she still found herself waking up in the middle of the night. The phone buzzed, bringing her attention to the fact that it was only 8:02 am. She turned the phone over and saw a text from Casey.

8:02 am ~ Casey

Hey, Girl. Just want to let you know we are standing on the Word of God. Love you and remember all things work together for good to them that love God, to them who are called according to His

purpose. Romans 8:28 Because you love
Him this will work out for your good.
Please let me know as soon as you get the
news. Love You.

A tear escaped LaShonda's eye as she looked at the text. She needed that reminder. Throughout the last couple of days her friends and church family had really surrounded her. Closing her eyes, she recited the scripture that she had plastered everywhere and had worked it into her daily confession: Isaiah 54:17. *No weapon formed against me shall prosper.* She opened her eyes and glanced at her phone to see she still had not received a call. Turning around and looking at the computer screen, she decided to start working on some cases.

When LaShonda looked up from the computer screen, she realized it was almost lunch time and still no call. She had gotten a few calls, but none were from her doctor's office. Some people say no news was good news, but no news right now was driving her up the wall.

"Let me go ahead and take my morning break." Getting up from her desk, LaShonda went downstairs and filled up her water bottle. She managed to laugh and talk with some of the cafeteria staff. She was catching the elevator back upstairs when she realized she had left her phone. Out of all days she left her phone on her desk, today was not the day to do so. She got off the elevator, made a bee line to her desk, grabbed her phone, and still saw no missed call. Letting out a sigh as she placed the phone back on her desk and started to unlock her computer.

She glanced down when she felt her phone vibrate and saw the caller ID was displaying Palmetto. She hesitated to answer because Palmetto was the name of the hospital system in town, and she did not know anyone who was in the hospital. Curiosity made her decision to pick up the phone.

"Hello, is this Ms. Barnes?" "Yes, who is this?"

"Hi, my name is Tiffany Anderson, and I am one of the Nurse Navigators here at Palmetto."

"Ok, how can I help you?"

Tiffany cleared her throat and said, "On Friday, you went and got a biopsy of your breast, and I was calling you with your results."

"Yes, I been waiting all morning for this call. What were the results?"

"Ms. Barnes, the tests results are in, and I am sorry to say that it came back that you are in the early stages of Breast Cancer."

Chapter 11

LaShonda had just finished setting up the layout of the food throughout her kitchen. It was the singles ministry's monthly meeting, and it was her turn to host. Planning this month's meeting made her feel like what she had experienced a few weeks ago was part of a dream; more like a nightmare. She could not believe what she had experienced.

When Tiffany from the medical center started rambling off so much information, LaShonda got lost and stuck on the word *Cancer*. When Tiffany had finished rambling and she had started asking questions to LaShonda but received no response.

"Ms. Barnes... Ms. Barnes? Are you still there?"

LaShonda took a deep breath, trying not to cry.

"Yes, I am here." "Ms. Barnes, I want you to breathe."

LaShonda took another deep breath and then another one until she felt life coming back into her. The words that Tiffany had said to her had sucked the life out of her. She snapped back into reality when she heard Tiffany's voice.

"Ms. Barnes Ms. Barnes, I know I have given you a lot of information, but we have to get you set up with your first appointment with the surgeon."

"Surgeon?" The little bit of calmness that had crept into her had quickly disappeared within a flash.

"I have to meet with a surgeon?" She felt anxiety and panic overwhelming her.

"The area that has been identified; we need to have that removed. So, we must get you scheduled with a surgeon and then we need to get you scheduled for an MRI and genetic testing…"

The doorbell snapped her out of her thoughts. Placing the plates that she had just gotten out of her pantry, she went to the door to open them, finding David with bags in his hands.

"Hey, Shonda," David said. Looking at LaShonda, he could tell that something was wrong. "Is everything ok?"

She stepped back to allow him in.

"Everything is fine. Why are you here so early?" "I told you that I would bring the desserts. Are you sure everything ok?"

"Yeah, you can go and place them on the table. Let me go in the back and change my clothes."

"Shonda…"

Before David could question LaShonda any further, she disappeared down the hallway to her room and closed the door. Part of him wanted to barge in there and demand that she tells him what was wrong. He loved her and it was tearing him up inside that she was going through something and did not feel comfortable enough to tell him. He remembered how he heard the Holy Spirit tell him that she was going to be an immense help to him. And when he got home that day, he called his dad and told him what he had heard the Holy Spirit say to him.

His dad had prayed for it and after a few weeks his dad called him and told him to be patient with LaShonda. And since she had been hurt and if David was to rush too fast, then she would balk. He said that she was like a wild horse, used to roaming along, not because of wanting to but because of desertion. She did not know how it was like to be a part of the herd; that it was protection in a herd. So, David had been trying to do just that. He had developed a deep love for Shonda and could pick up when something was wrong with her, and it had been more than one time where she had picked up something was wrong with him.

"Lord, I do not know what is wrong with her, but I serve an all-knowing God who will never leave us comfortless. Lord, comfort her, let her know that she is not

alone in this. Give her peace, Lord." David looked at the still closed door. "Amen."

Gripping the bags with desserts, he proceeded to walk into her dining room to set up the dessert table.

❀

❧ LATER THAT EVENING

The night had gone by without a hitch. As usual, the meeting had run over, and her house did not clear until after midnight. She did not know why but every time they had a meeting at her house, it always let out late. She was so thankful that David showed up when he did. David sat next to LaShonda and kept her calm. Whenever she was feeling some type of way, she could feel David praying for her. She laughed and enjoyed the conversation but inside, she just wanted to be alone and cry her eyes out. It was what she had done for the past few weeks. This week alone she had been to three doctor's appointments.

Glancing at the cabinet where she put the mail, she saw the thick white envelope that she was given at her first appointment. Tiffany, her nurse navigator, had shown her the contents of that package before she put the information in it and sealed the envelope that had her name on it. Most nights, she was ok until she looked at that cabinet. It was like seeing that white envelope made what she thought was a nightmare into reality. But whenever she felt like she was about to cry, she felt

David's hand grip hers underneath the table. He never stopped talking or laughing, but he silently told her she was not alone.

Before everyone left, Casey made everyone clean up. Casey was one of the few that knew the truth of what was going on with LaShonda.

A few minutes after David had arrived earlier, she heard the doorbell ring. When she opened her door, a pair of strong arms pulled her into an embrace.

"Girl, I told you we could have had this meeting at my house."

As they both shed tears, LaShonda softly said, "This week has been nothing but normal so any bit of normalcy that I can have I want to keep it."

Casey held her in her arms and rocked LaShonda back and forth until LaShonda finally said, "Okay. Let us get this party going."

LaShonda got off the floor, wiping her eyes as she went into her closet and chose a soft jersey dress with some fuzzy socks. Anyone who knew LaShonda knew she hated wearing shoes. Casey took one look at her when she came out of the bathroom and laughed.

"Girl, at least get some fuzzy socks that match the dress." As LaShonda went back into the closet, Casey sat there still staring at the closet door. LaShonda had been through so much and even though they have been friends for over thirty years, Casey always looked at her as the epitome of strength.

Casey had witnessed the craziness of LaShonda's foster mother when she called, and her mother was cussing her out in the background. LaShonda would come to school and sleep in class, and no one knew the reasons why. Casey found out after they became partners on a school project. Casey had called one night, and LaShonda's mother had picked up and told her that she had kicked LaShonda out. Casey begged her momma to go over to make sure LaShonda was ok. When they got there, they found LaShonda sitting on the top step of their house, holding herself, trying to keep warm. Casey's mom let LaShonda spend that night with them and from that point on. Anytime during the school year LaShonda needed a place to sleep, Casey's mom did not hesitate to open her doors. Casey's mom had remodeled her room and put a day bed in her room so LaShonda could have a place to sleep during those nights.

Casey looked at her friend, knowing what she was going through. She stood there, praying silently that God gave not only LaShonda strength, but them as well. She did not know what she would do if something happened to her friend.

❀

❧ LATER THAT NIGHT

LaShonda heard her phone ring, and she made her way to the living room to retrieve her phone. Picking it up, she saw it was a text from David.

1:02 am

I do not know what is going on with you but know you are never in this alone. Love you. Here when you are ready to talk, MY SUNSHINE.

Tears formed in her eyes. David had been such a huge help, but she knew that she did not need to involve David in this. She did not know what she would be encountering. The doctor had told her that based on the genetic testing, it was a possibility that she would have to have her entire breast removed. She did not want to involve David with that. No way she could involve him in this. She was so torn because she wanted to tell him, but she quickly shook those thoughts out of her head. No. She could not involve David. Turning the lights off as she headed to her bedroom, she prayed it was not another sleepless night.

Chapter 12

❦ 2 WEEKS LATER

LaShonda was at her ninth appointment that month. She had an average of two appointments a week since her diagnosis. Sitting in the cold room, she reflected on everything that she had gone through in the previous weeks. The genetic testing had come back with no family history of breast cancer. It was a big relief to her because it meant no major surgery. After talking to her pastors, she decided to go ahead and do the lumpectomy and radiation. She had been given three options by Amanda, her genetic counselor. The first was a lumpectomy with radiation and five-10 years of Tamoxifen; a single or double mastectomy with tamoxifen; with reconstruction later or reconstruction could be done immediately after the mastectomy. She was ok with her decision after researching each option. The door opened and she watched as Dr.

Mason walked in with Tiffany. She released a nervous sigh. Dr. Mason had been assigned as her surgeon and this was her third meeting with him.

"Ms. Barnes, how are you?"

"I'm ok." LaShonda said nervously.

Dr. Mason hopped up on the examination table and faced her. "I heard you have some questions for me, so you can finalize your decision."

"Yes, I think I want to go over the lumpectomy and wanted to know how long is that procedure and typically the length of healing times." LaShonda wanted to know how soon she would be able to go back to work and get back to a life of normalcy. She was ready to finish this and put this far behind her.

Sighing, Dr. Mason looked at Tiffany, who in return looked at him.

"I had a feeling you were not fully listening to what I was saying when I heard that you were considering a lumpectomy. Ms. Barnes, I can do a lumpectomy but the area that I am going to have to remove is too large, so you really do not qualify for a lumpectomy."

LaShonda twisted her face as she took in what he was saying.

"What do you mean I do not qualify? I do not understand. I thought as long as the genetic test came back saying I didn't have a history of breast cancer that I qualified."

Getting off the bed, Dr. Mason asked for his tablet to be brought to him by one of the nurses. The nurse came in and handed him his tablet. He pulled up her imaging on his tablet from the radiology report.

"Ms. Barnes, this is your breast. The cancer is in the frontal part of the breast so I will have to remove the entire frontal area almost due to the size. The area that will need to be removed is 7.2 cm, which is about 3 to 3 ½ inches of tissue removed. You remember that I told you we will have to continue removing tissue until we get clear margins." He continued once he saw her shake her head *yes*.

"Well, that is without obtaining clear margins. I am sorry you do not qualify for a lumpectomy. I am recommending a single or double mastectomy with reconstruction later due to your age."

"This is too much." LaShonda said, looking at the floor.

"I know but I need to know are you okay with the plan to remove just your left breast?"

"It doesn't seem like I have a choice."

"I am sorry, Ms. Barnes, but it is for the best. Tiffany, let us get her set up with the plastic surgeon as soon as possible." Dr. Mason gave her hand a squeeze before he excused himself from the room.

"Are you ok, Ms. Barnes?"

"No, but I will be. Will you be calling me later today to give me this new appointment?"

"I will if they have not done it by the time we leave from here. I know that this is a lot of information, but you are making the right decision, and I am quite sure they are going to make your appointment with Dr. Wise. He is good. What day do you see your oncologist?"

Hearing those words sent shivers through her. "Thursday afternoon."

"Ok, do you have any other questions before we head out?"

Not trusting her voice to speak she shook her head as she gathered her things to leave the room. She made it to her car and immediately dialed Momma Glenda.

"What happened?"

"They told me that I have to have a mastectomy; that I am not eligible for a lumpectomy." When silence met her, she did not wait for her to respond.

"This is not what we were praying for. Why does it seem like it is getting worse? I am not blaming God but dang, why?" LaShonda broke down on the phone before the call ended. When Momma Glenda tried to call LaShonda back, it immediately went to voicemail.

❋

"Lord, we need you." Glenda said, turning to Bishop Horry. "Did she say where she is? We could get her."

"No, she hung up and now is sending her calls to voicemail." Glenda walked over and sat beside Bishop. "I don't know what to say."

"We are going to have to keep her in faith and remind her that she is not alone. Come on.

Let us pray." Holding hands, they went into prayer.

Chapter 13

"Where is Shonda?" David asked Bishop Horry as he was sitting in the front of the church. Most of the members and visitors had left. He had intentionally waited for everyone to leave so that he could talk to Bishop Horry.

"Shonda is not feeling well. Hopefully, she will be back here on next Wednesday." But Bishop did not sound so sure. They had a group chat that everyone was a part of.

Everyone had tried to reach out to LaShonda since Tuesday, but she was nowhere to be found.

She was gone and if it was not for the text that she had sent Sunday's morning letting them know that she was ok but just needed a break, they were going to go to the police and report her missing.

It was just an uncomplicated text.

8:02 am - Shonda

> *Hey, I know you all have been trying to contact me but honestly, I just do not want to talk. I am tired and I just need a break from everything. I did go to all my appointments and left after each appointment. I am ok, no, I do not want to hurt myself, but I am trying to decipher what is going on and right now, I just want to be alone. Please respect that. I will be home soon. Love you all.*

"She is sick. I been texting her all weekend." David said with a concerned look on his face.

"Son, if you care for her, pray for her. She needs it." And with that, Bishop got out of his seat and made his way to the back, leaving a stunned David in the sanctuary by himself.

❀

❧ LaShonda

LaShonda drove slower than normal. This week had been a whirlwind and while she understood what she was going to have to endure, she needed to really comprehend what was going to happen to her. She reached up and rubbed her left breast. The doctor had called, and everything was scheduled four weeks from Wednesday. She had four weeks to transform her house to accommodate her post surgery lifestyle.

Her phone started to buzz. She knew it was probably one of the crew. She laughed as she remembered the text exchange that had happened between them after she had sent them the morning text to let them know that she would not be in church.

8:03 am – Michael Jr.

Man, at least tell us where you at? You are being single and all we need to know.

8:03 am - Trina

Love you and here for you.

8:03 am – Shell

You know where we are but if I do not see you soon, just know I still have connections with my FBI friend. IJS

8:04 am – *Momma Glenda*

You all stop it! Shonda, we are here for you. Let us be here for you. Love you and WE WILL SEE YOU SOON. If you get back in tonight, stop by the house. It is third Sunday, and you know how we do it.

8:05 am – *Daniel*

Lord, you got Momma on here trying to sound hip. LOL! On the real, where you at?

Daniel acted like he did not know where she was when, honestly, he was the only one that knew where she was. When he had called, she picked up and tried to sound okay, thinking he did not know what had just happened. However, when he asked how she was feeling, she knew he was aware of her diagnosis and burst out crying. Daniel had come to her house and even helped her produce the plan. He knew that she needed time alone without everyone crowding her.

So, she made it seem like to anyone who would look for her that she had left town. She had rented a car and left her car at the car rental place. She knew her family loved her, but she always had to be a couple of steps ahead of them. She stayed at the bed and breakfast on the outskirts of town. The plush bed had pulled her into a deep sleep that she had needed. She had not slept since her diagnosis.

As she turned onto her street, she noticed a car parked in front of her house. Pulling into her driveway, she realized it was David. She turned the key, killed the engine, and waited for the tap on her window she knew was coming. LaShonda unbuckled her seatbelt and pulled her key out of the ignition, causing her lights to come on in the car. David immediately opened her door.

"Hey."

LaShonda looked up into David's eyes and could see the concern in his face. David had texted her all weekend and she had not responded.

"Hey," LaShonda said, as she got out the car with her pocketbook and overnight bag. She stepped out of the way so David could close the door. When he closed the door, she leaned back on her car and waited for David to speak but he did not. Instead, he grabbed her keys from her hands and led her towards the house. He quickly activated her car alarm as he unlocked her front door and let her in. He was on her heels as LaShonda instructed the alert to have her Mimi app turn on the light in her living room. She walked to the couch, dropped her bag in an empty chair, and curled up on the couch as she waited for David to speak. He came and sat down beside her.

"Shonda, what is wrong?" Tears started to form in her eyes and the next thing she knew they were falling. David pulled her into his arms and rocked her.

"You can tell me."

LaShonda got up and grabbed some tissues from the tissue box on the other side of the room. She needed a moment to pull herself together. She cried and slept all weekend. She was tired of just thinking about it any longer and she blurted it out, "It's cancer."

"Cancer?" An astonished David repeated the words that LaShonda had just said. She returned to her seat and watched him digest the words that she relayed. He swallowed the lump that had formed in his throat and looked at her.

"What type?" "Breast Cancer." "What stage?"

"They think they caught it early, but I won't know until I have surgery."

Hope crept across David's face as he said, "That's good… Wait, you have to have surgery?"

LaShonda nodded. "The spot is too big for a lumpectomy and so they have to remove my breast."

"Shonda…"

"No, David. It is best that you go on with your life. This is about to be too much to ask of you."

"I am not going anywhere. We will go through this together."

"No, David. You should be with someone who can give you children. They are taking my breast, and they are putting me on medicine so I cannot get pregnant. I am almost forty and I am going to be on that medicine for a minimum of five years and you know what else?" Not giving him time to respond, she continued. "It is still a chance that I may have to do chemo. Yes, chemotherapy. They said if they find even a millimeter of cancer that has upgraded, I have to have chemo."

As David stood up and gathered her in her arms, LaShonda tried to fight David's embrace for a moment, but with no energy left to fight, she finally allowed herself to be comforted by him.

❀

❧ AN HOUR LATER

Leaving out of her bedroom, LaShonda left her bedroom to find David in the living room with sandwiches and drinks.

"I didn't know if you had eaten or not."

"Thanks."

She and David sat on the floor, Indian style, and ate in silence. After finishing the last bite of her sandwich, she looked up and caught David eyeing her.

"I knew I shouldn't have told you," LaShonda said, trying to get up, but David grabbed her hand, holding her in place.

"Why wouldn't you?"

"Because I didn't want you looking at me with that look." "What look?"

"That look of pity. Everyone has been looking at me with that look ever since I told them.

I do not want your pity, David I need your strength."

David held his hands up to silence LaShonda, and she sat back down. She waited for what seemed like minutes before he looked her dead in the eye and spoke.

"I am not looking at you in pity. I am looking at you in admiration. You have been going through all this and yet to a person on the outside looking in, you would think that everything is ok. I admire your strength and your resilience. And if it is my strength that you need, you have it. I am not leaving you. I am here for you."

"Why?"

"Why not?"

"No one else wanted to."

"What are you talking about?" David said.

"My parents left me at DSS. I have a foster family not even thirty miles away and when I called them to tell them what was going on, they said, 'Ok, we will talk later.' I have not heard from them since. People are so quick to walk away when I need them to stay."

LaShonda angrily swiped at the tears that had fallen on her cheeks.

"I cannot fix who walked away from you in the past, but I can show you who is going to *stay* with you in your present and in your future. I am not going anywhere and while you may have begged others to stay, all you have to do is ask me."

She closed her eyes, letting the words that David had just spoken to her wash over her. She felt his hand calmly rub her hand as he waited for her to give him her response.

"David?"

"Yes?"

"I want you to stay."

David leaned forward and kissed LaShonda's forehead. The words that his father had said echoed in the back of his head. He was glad he took the time and allowed her to discover who he was and that she could trust him. Pulling her into his arms he rocked her to sleep.

Chapter 14

The next morning, LaShonda awoke in her bed to the smell of breakfast cooking. She wiped the sleep out of her eyes and pulled herself up in the bed. She still had the same clothes on that she had on last night. Smiling, she realized David must have put her to bed. Getting up, she walked into the bathroom and quickly washed up. She had taken the day off because she was meeting with her surgeons again to go over final details of the surgery. She would work until the week of her surgery and then she would go on FMLA. Getting out of the shower, she felt good, probably because it was the first time in a long time that she had slept through an entire night. She knew it had a lot to do with David. She did not even remember going to sleep.

She changed into her clothes and walked into her living room where she saw that David had obviously slept on the couch, despite her having a guest room bedroom. She stood still, enjoying hearing his singing coming from the kitchen. When the doors opened, David came out of the kitchen carrying two plates.

"Good morning, my Sunshine."

Blushing, Shonda looked at the ground and then looked back up at him.

"Good morning." David stood, waiting for her to say his nickname. It was as though the air between them became still and then she added, "My Love."

David did not realize that he had been holding his breath. Placing the plates on the table, he said, "Have a seat. Breakfast will be ready in a few minutes."

"What's on the menu?" Lashonda asked.

"French toast and bacon." David said proudly.

"You know how to cook?" Lashonda looked at him surprised.

"Yes, I do. Why are you looking at me surprised?" "Anytime you bring anything, it is always store brought."

"Well, most of the things that you all tell me what to bring, I cannot cook, but I can cook. I can make a mean box cake, and I do some surprisingly good pies."

"A mean box cake... I am shocked. Thank you for cooking breakfast for me... I mean, us."

"Anytime, my Sunshine."

Going back into the kitchen, he brought out a platter of eggs, bacon, and French toast with juice and water. Placing everything on the table and sitting down, David reached out for Shonda's hands and went into prayer.

"Lord, thank you for this day and allowing us to partake in this breakfast. I ask that you strengthen both of us during this time. Help me be what she needs me to be in this hour and get out of her what you need to get out of her in this hour. And even though we know you are a God that can cancel this, we join our faith together and we will yet continue to give you the praise. No matter how you bring forth her healing. In Jesus's name. Amen."

"Amen. Thank you."

"You do not have to thank me. What do you have planned today?" "I've got to meet with my surgeons today."

"Ok, I hope you do not mind me tagging alone. I took today off." "David, you don't…"

"I want to. Shonda, look at me…" When LaShonda peered at him, he said, "**We** are fighting this. Whatever you need, I am here, ok?"

Giving a hesitating breath, Shonda nodded.

"So can I come with you today?" LaShonda again nodded, and David squeezed her hand. They went back to eating their breakfast and David started telling her about service.

❧ LATER THAT DAY

When David and LaShonda came back into the house after her appointments with her surgeons, David hugged her and told her to go and lay down. She went into the den where she sat to watch TV but soon found herself falling asleep. David had taken her to both of her appointments. She was shocked by how much he was involved.

He had stayed up most of the night researching Breast Cancer, and her doctors were excited to see that she had brought someone with her to be her support. The doctors were concerned about her not having the proper support because she had come to all her previous appointments by herself. He assured them that her support system was strong and that she was far from having to go through this alone. Smiling, she closed her eyes and went to sleep.

David peeked into the den and saw LaShonda had fallen asleep. Grabbing one of the throws that she had on the couch, he covered her up and walked into the living room. Picking up the phone, he called his father. He had called his father that night before and had spoken to his dad for a good three hours after he had put LaShonda in her bed. As David told his dad what she was going through, he broke down after he uttered the words 'cancer.' His dad and his mom had stayed on the phone with him until they made sure he was okay.

He had never really had to walk with someone through sickness. When his dad asked him if was, he going to stay, he told his dad that he was not going to leave her now. For some strange reason, he felt as though it made his dad proud to hear that.

His dad picked up the phone on the third ring, immediately telling him to hold on while he got his mother. David heard his father say, "Okay, son. I got you on speaker."

"Baby how is Shonda doing and how did the visit go today?" his mother's voice came through the phone with worry.

"She is scheduled for surgery a month from Wednesday. She had two doctor's appointments today, both with the surgeons. One with the doctor who will do the removal and the plastic surgeon. This just seems like a bad dream."

"Has she put down her deposit for her surgery?" his dad asked.

"No, but when she was leaving the first surgeon's office, the lady in the office said that this surgery is over thirty thousand dollars."

"What type of insurance does she have?"

"She has a high deductible plan. When she was checking out, she asked for her bill. It was $268.32. I took care it."

"That is good. Son, me, and your mother have been talking. Let Shonda know that we got $1000 on her surgery."

"What?"

"Yes, Shonda is family, and we also know that you were planning to propose to her."

David thought about the diamond ring that was in his glove compartment and that he was planning to propose the same weekend that she was going to have surgery. He was brought back to reality when he heard LaShonda waking up.

"Hey, who are you on the phone with?" she asked.

"Mom and Dad. Hey. Shonda just woke up. Let me put you two on speaker."

"Hey, baby. How are you?"

"I am fine. So, David told you what is going on?"

"Yes, and we are praying for you. We know God is a healer," David's father said.

"Yes sir." Sitting down on the couch beside David, she lowered her head to his shoulder, and he leaned his head on top of hers.

"David was telling us about your doctor's visits today."

"Yes," LaShonda picked up her phone and saw that she had a voicemail, quickly going to the app that makes the voicemail a text, she started to read the message. David looked concerned at her.

"Is everything ok?"

Releasing a sigh, LaShonda glanced up and nodded her head *yes*.

"I did not realize my phone was silent. I have to go get an EKG a week prior to surgery."

"For what?" David asked, looking at her.

"I do not know... it was a message from the scheduling center calling to get it scheduled. It is after five. I will call them tomorrow."

"Shonda, we are here for you. We know that you have your church family there with you, but we are here with you also. We going to come up for your surgery."

"You all don't have to," Shonda said, while whipping her eyes.

"We know that we do not have to, but it is a fact that we *want* to. Now Shonda, how much do you have to put down for this surgery?"

"I do not know. I will not know until I register for surgery."

"Ok, well, we are going to help you with it, and we are not accepting *no* for an answer.

Love you dear and we will speak soon. Call us if you need anything."

When David's parents hung up, both David and LaShonda sat in silence. "Your parents are amazing."

"I know, and they mean that. After I put you to bed last night, I called them and told them everything. Shonda, I do not know what is going to happen, but I just want to let you know that I do not plan to leave you."

LaShonda sat up and turned to look at David, taking his hand and squeezing it. "For once, I believe this. Thank you for just being you."

Epilogue

"It is almost time," the attendant came to the door and spoke.

LaShonda stood, looking at herself in the mirror. It was her wedding day. She could not believe that so much had occurred on this day in July just a year ago. On this day she was diagnosed with breast cancer. Her entire life as she knew it had changed. From going back and forth to doctors' appointments to having the surgery.

Due to some complications after surgery, they had not been able to take out the drain as they had hoped and LaShonda had to wear the drain for almost a month. Once the drain was removed, she was able to start the reconstruction process. She went through almost three months of fills before she was able to finally start the reconstruction surgeries. Four surgeries later, she was coming out of her plastic surgeon's office when she was encountered by someone singing and when she looked towards the music, there was David down on one knee with his family and their church family behind him. It was there he asked her to marry him.

He chose that day for them to wed because he wanted to give her new memories of happiness and joy on this day. Her bridal court all squealed as she turned around. LaShonda was adorned in an off the shoulder beaded, ivory A-line dress. One of the elders at the church was walking her down the aisle. Her bridesmaids, her maid, and matron of honor gave her a quick squeeze before walking one by one out of the door. One of the members of the media team came and handed her a mic. No one outside of her bridal party knew what she had planned to do. Not many knew she could sing; not singing where she would record a record but enough to hold a tune. The attendant opened the door and motioned for her to start.

"Hello everyone. I know this is a shock for many of you to hear me, but I realized that I have not really told you all something… Let me tell you why I love him." Shonda then began to sing a song that she had written with the help of a song writer. When she finished the song with, "I Love you, Baby," the doors opened, and she stepped into the sanctuary. There was not a dry eye in the house and when she looked for her son to be husband, at first, she did not see him.

Panic started to overcome her, but then she saw his best man, Brad, reach down and help him get up off the floor. David was in tears. LaShonda smiled because they had made a bet that whoever did not cry first won the bet. It appeared she was the winner.

As she walked down the aisle, she began to cry. Last year, God had not only healed her body from cancer, but He had given her a man that was specifically molded just for her. After the mastectomy, her oncologist told her it was Stage 1 and when she heard that, she was bracing herself for the treatment plan but then her oncologist said, "We caught it early, and as of today, you are CANCER FREE." While she still had to do hormonal therapy for five years, upon hearing those words, she sat there and cried. When the doctor had her nurse get David after her examination and when he saw her tears, he immediately started telling her that she was not in this by herself, and he was going to help her fight.

He was in the middle of promising to shave his head when LaShonda placed a hand over his lips and told him that she was CANCER FREE. While she could not move around that much due to the surgery, David about tore the room up shouting. When he finished, he grabbed her hands and began to pray and give God praise for what HE had Done. As she looked into David's eyes as he stood across from her, she knew two things: one, David was definitely heaven sent, and two, he had brought her sunshine on a cloudy day. The cancer diagnosis made her realize to stop living in the past and to live each moment.

❀

❧ LATER THAT EVENING

"Mrs. Johnson, can I have this dance?" David stood with his hand extended to LaShonda.

She had just finished dancing with his little nephew.

"Of course, my husband." As David brought her onto the floor, they started to dance. "Are you ok?"

"I am more than ok."

"I wanted to make sure; I know we invited your family and a lot of them didn't-." David was unable to finish his sentence as LaShonda kissed him.

"Baby, one thing I learned going through everything that I... I mean, we went through, is that family are the ones who stood with me, checked on me, took me back and forth to the doctors, etc. That is my family. I still love my foster family, but I am not concerned about what they do and do not do anymore."

David leaned in to kiss her. "We love you and we got you. You are Mrs. Johnson now." They leaned into each other as her favorite Ledisi's song *Anything for You* started to play. As they danced, they started singing the song to each other. But abruptly, the DJ stopped the song.

"I am so sorry. It looks as though we are having some technical difficulties. Give me a few minutes," the DJ yelled from the booth. Then a voice said, "Well, I guess it pays to have the real thing."

Breaking their embrace, LaShonda turned and looked dead at Ledisi standing on stage.

She started screaming. She could not believe it.

"Your husband invited me here today; he said that this was your song and asked could I perform it."

"You are my sunshine on a cloudy day. Thank you for making my world more colorful by taking my last name." David said into her ear as his arms encircled around a shocked LaShonda. She turned into his arms as Ledisi began to sing. While LaShonda knew no one was perfect, she knew that she and David would spend the rest of their lives showing how much they meant to one another.

Sunshine On a Cloudy Day
Book 1 of the Day Series

The End

But the path of the righteous
is like the light of dawn,
That shines brighter and
brighter until the full day.

Proverbs 4: 18 KJV

www.ingramcontent.com/pod-product-compliance
Ingram Content Group UK Ltd.
Pitfield, Milton Keynes, MK11 3LW, UK
UKHW021430240125
4283UKWH00041B/543